A Letter From Lydia

by

Mollie Chappell

Dales Large Print Books
Long Preston, North Yorkshire,
England.

British Library Cataloguing in Publication Data.

SV '99

Chappell, Mollie
A letter from Lydia

A catalogue record for this book is
available from the British Library

ISBN 1-85389-868-6 pbk

First published in Great Britain by Collins, 1974

Copyright © 1974 by Mollie Chappell

Cover illustration © Melvyn Warren-Smith by arrangement
with P.W.A. International Ltd.

The moral right of the author has been asserted

Published in Large Print 1999 by arrangement with P.O'N
Carden as Power of Attorney for Mrs M.B. Chappell

Dales Large Print is an imprint of
Library Magna Books Ltd.
Printed and bound in Great Britain by
T.J. International Ltd., Cornwall, PL28 8RW.

1

December at the Cape is glorious, the Season in Southern Africa. Those who can afford it, and many who can't, make for it. Blue sky, blue seas, beaches and beauty. It is perfection.

Lydia Farmer should have been happy but found that scenery, warmth and sophisticated living were not enough. She was lonely and not happy. Her suite in the hotel was luxurious, the sitting-room filled with flowers bought that morning by Lydia herself at the Flower Market. A pretence at housekeeping? Maybe.

Times without number, not only here at Cape Town, she had rebuked herself for feeling miserable, reminding herself how many women would like to change places with her. It doesn't really help to be cross with yourself. Understandably, you are biased.

It was near to Christmas, and if you are lonely, perhaps understandably the season of goodwill and exaggerated friendliness is the least likely to help. Lydia Farmer was not only lonely at Christmas, though. Easter, the Feast of Saint Michael and All Angels, Columbus Day, U.S.A., it could happen.

Don't mope, she scolded. There are things to do. Read the brochure. *Write a brochure.* Watch cricket. Go racing. Kirstenbosch and Groot Constantia. The view from the top of the mountain.

I have walked and watched, motored and stared.

Do it again. Paint a view. Plot a book. God knows there are enough people plotting books if not painting the view. She had a feeling she might not finish the view or the book.

You are hopeless.

Shop for next Christmas. You bought presents for this year in Singapore, nine months ago.

You should be ashamed.

Oh, she was. This was the trouble. Harder-skinned, hedonistic, she would be like the rest.

Why did you come, then? Because last Christmas, in Switzerland, when I asked myself where I should be this Christmas, Cape Town, I said, and I stuck to it.

Her mother, Syb, was in New York. 'Come here for Christmas and bring your young man,' Syb had said when she telephoned, the week before, throwing out the feeler. Lydia said no, she would stay in Cape Town, and did not mention a young man. There was a short silence until Syb said, and it was all she did say, 'Perhaps you are right. It's snowing here.'

She has a right to get impatient with me, to wash her hands of me, Lydia thought. I am certainly not making much effort as daughter of the popular, scintillating, energetic Syb Farmer. An expensive education at one of Britain's top schools, then on to Switzerland. A year in Italy. I haven't done much with all that. Sometimes I wonder if I should not have been happier if I had been born to inherit a corner shop tucked away somewhere where I served the chocolate bars and the jelly babies, listened to the customers' gossip, sympathized or rejoiced, as it came. My fund of sympathy, which I am certain I possess and which I grieve at not using, would have been handy there.

But that is just a dream. The truth is that I am Syb's daughter and Toby's daughter. Syb knows everyone. Toby meets hardly anyone but from choice because he is too lazy to make the effort. But both are happy because it is what they want.

Is it that I don't know what I want? But I do. I tried to tell my mother once.

Today's blacker than usual mood had its origins in what had happened the night before when a young man had asked her to dine and dance. He was a friend of her mother's and admired her mother very much. He started out by being pleasant to Syb's daughter but by the end of the meal both knew that if by chance they met again they would prefer to nip up a side street rather than talk.

He had liked talking about himself and, like conceited young men, talking and day dreaming were in equal proportions. He spattered his conversation with 'If only—' and 'If I had the chance—' He didn't mean any of it. But Lydia, pleasant girl that she was, took him at his face value, listened to him and took his posturings for truth. When he said, 'What do you think?' she told him what she thought, told him what appeared to be wrong with him and how he could put it right, until the conceited creature could stand it no longer and said, 'Oh, shut up. Stop making me over. You've done everything except wipe my nose for me and say "Blow".' Cruelly he told her he could take this sort of thing from her mother. 'But you want to get a bit of life in yourself, before you dish out the advice.'

Lydia supposed he was right. Perhaps she did overdo it when people asked her advice because it happened so seldom. It went to her head. She blushed now when she remembered how earnestly she had advised him what to do. 'You need a family of your own to boss up,' he said. 'A man and six kids.'

Indeed, she did.

To look at, she resembled Syb. Black hair and eyes, creamy skin. Tall and elegantly dressed. Here it ended. A superficial resemblance. Lydia did not have Syb's glow. She was a more honest person.

Perhaps though, when it did happen, when she fell in love, she too would be beautiful as Syb was beautiful. The difference between them would be, if love was the key word, that Syb loved Syb. Lydia would love another.

She was a quiet young woman, one who, at a party, would be left in a corner watching a girl nowhere near as good-looking, but filled to the brim with self confidence and vivacity who was surrounded by men.

What is it that attracts? Is it self confidence, that certainty within one that others recognize and come to warm themselves by?

Is it the other side of the coin, an out-going sympathy which marks you as the recipient for the life story?

To take the first. Lydia was not over blessed with self confidence. Syb had been an overpowering force to grow up with while Toby hadn't cared.

Interest in others? She was filled with it. What she needed, indeed, was to channel her love when she would be a wonderful wife and mother. She knew, better than anyone, that she was wasting time threshing around wondering where to go and what to do. She longed to have a direction to make for.

Leafing through the magazine she held, her eye was taken by a picture of an English December scene. Pale sky, frozen water, black bizarre-shaped branches. *'And no birds sing,'* she said aloud. Winter. Guaranteed to moisten the exile's eye in some sunny clime. He would look at it and tell himself he longed to be back there, stepping out along the ridge at the top of the valley, the ground hard beneath his feet, the air too cold for snow. Ah, nostalgia. Then, sighing, he might put the picture away from him and go down to the beach and sunbathe. Joyfully.

Over the past years Lydia Farmer had become peripatetic, fortunate enough to have the money to take her wherever she wished to go. She believed she might be coming to the end of such places, what would remain would be the second eleven or see a place again. Fortunate, indeed. Yet here she sat, mooning over an artist's impression of a frozen English scene. A couple of these, he might have said, and I can afford to spend Christmas in South Africa!

England.

I can always go home.

See, I still call it home.

Of course I do. I was born there and went to school there. My father lives there.

So her mind see-sawed, she thought forward and she thought back, here on her own in the room while down on the beach those people who did give a

11

thought for Britain in December probably pitied it.

Lydia thought of Syb and of Toby and of what they had made or not made of their lives together, and how she Lydia, their only child, came to be here in this favoured spot dreaming of frozen pipes and chilblains.

Her mother was born Sybilla Johnson, and born with a silver spoon.

Syb's father made money, then married a woman with money. He said you can never have too much of it. There were lashings of the stuff. Both dead now. Grandmother Johnson left her money to Syb. Grandfather left all his to Lydia.

Syb's mother had died when Syb was in her teens so that she knew early she was an heiress and acted accordingly, being a flirt and capricious. But she was so pretty and so attractive, most of her flaws were overlooked. She was a sought after girl and not only by the fortune hunters though they were there in plenty. Her father spoiled her and gave her whatever she wanted.

When she met Toby Farmer she wanted him. Toby was still in uniform when Syb met him, tall, fair, very English, as they say, a girl's dream of a hero. Syb made a dead set at him. Her father made her wait at least until Toby was out of uniform. They they were married.

But once back in civilian life, sloth took over Toby and did it completely. Perhaps, in the last five years, he had had enough action to suit him. Whatever the cause, he was for the quiet life from now on. The quiet life, the country life. Syb could provide it so he married her. He was fond of her, he thought she was a good sort, but he didn't love her. Love, deep emotions, inordinate affection meant effort, and Toby wasn't born for it. Syb soaked up admiration. He didn't give her this either. When she complained, he said she must be a fool not to know she was the most stunning girl around. What did she want him to tell her for?

They made a striking pair, she dark and vividly lovely, like a poppy, Toby tall and fair and good looking. Syb had seemed twice herself when measured against Toby, twice as dazzling, with more energy than usual. Perhaps this should have warned him there would be pitfalls later when her energy clashed with his laziness. Though

Toby had never brawled. When Syb went into her fishwife act and threw things, he only fielded them and put them safe from her. When she harangued him, he sat back and closed his eyes. It was the most irritating habit he had. He never knew how close he came to having both eyes blacked.

Before the marriage, Syb's father, with a Forsyte's reverence for property, bought a couple of houses near the country town of Wadden. Wadden is ringed by hills, pleasant, tree-covered, but with houses today on each hill. Then, there were just two houses on one hill. Old Johnson snapped both up. The one at the bottom, near the road, was snug and cosy. The one at the top, almost on the crest, had a fine view of the estuary and the sea beyond. He told Syb he would give her the house of her choice. She chose the bottom one. 'But don't give it to me,' she said. 'Give it to our first born as a christening gift.' Old Johnson did better. He gave Lydia, the first born, both houses.

When Syb and Toby divorced, six years to the day after they married, Syb left Toby in the house, saying it showed she

14

had some shred of feelings left for him because she was certain he would sleep on the Embankment rather than go to the trouble of looking for a house for himself. Besides, she didn't want it. She didn't want to live there ever again.

Living with Toby, Syb used to say, made her feel like Mrs Sisyphus. Rolling a stone uphill to have it roll back was akin to trying to make Toby do something, make an effort. Toby would tell Syb not to get frantic, years before the word became fashionable. Relax, he would say. We are the lucky ones. We toil not nor spin. No need. So make the most of it. She couldn't.

So Syb and Lydia left the house at the bottom of one of Wadden's hills, and before long Toby married Vida Kettle who had known him all their lives and who, though she had hidden the fact, adored him. To find herself Mrs Toby Farmer was a dream come true. Vida revelled in it. (It was only Syb, foolishly and childishly spiteful, who said she could imagine why Vida, with a name like Kettle, wanted to change it.) Toby and Vida had a daughter Ellie who was eighteen now. Lydia's half-sister. Toby was impartial towards the

15

girls, taking as little interest in Ellie as he did in Lydia.

Lydia saw her father occasionally but never at the house. In the early days Toby had made the effort to get to London when Syb and Lydia lived there. Once, Lydia had met him at Longchamps. At the Monte Carlo Rally. (If Toby could persuade a friend to make arrangements for some sporting event, he might go. He did arrange his own golf matches.)

Lydia liked him. It was impossible not to. Toby was still good-looking, still charming, a pleasant enough companion as long as you made no demands and knew he would leave you at the end of the day. But you never went to Toby if you were in trouble. It was a waste of time. Lydia wasn't keen on going to Syb, either, but for a different reason. Syb would demand to know why you had got into the mess, to start with. She might help but her methods seared your self esteem.

When Lydia was twenty, Syb asked what she meant to do with her life. But while Lydia took time to reply to so important a question, Syb lost patience and answered for her. She had a habit of doing this. While you were silent, choosing your words, she briskly told you what she thought you should say. If you demurred, she said, 'Well, why didn't you say so?'

'An antique shop,' Syb said. 'A gallery? Lots of girls doing this now. Your sort.' Lydia had fleetingly wondered what her sort was. Those who sported what she herself called The Knightsbridge Knot? The scarf tied on the chin, never, but never, beneath it.

She started to say, 'I'll tell you what I want—' But the telephone rang and Syb went to answer it and this was the moment of truth gone for ever. It never came back. Lydia never found she wanted to tell Syb a second time. For what she was going to say, five years ago, was that she wished above all to marry and to start a family, to have a house somewhere in the country, husband, kids, dogs. Cats, of course. She would spend her life looking after them and loving it. All this was what she was going to say but didn't.

That telephone call, the interruption, seemed to Lydia to mark a watershed in her relationship with her mother. It was the time when Lydia was certain that Connie Coles, who was telephoning, was more important to Syb than Syb's own

17

flesh and blood. Later, much later, Lydia found she had been right to think it. As a guess it was brilliant.

Connie Coles, born Maggie Mint in Manchester, had made a name for herself as an actress and *diseuse* in the States. Syb, on a visit to New York, which she always said was her favourite city, went to the theatre to see the acclaimed Miss Coles. When Connie appeared, Syb said aloud, 'Why it's Mag—' And was thrilled. Little shivers ran up and down her spine.

After the show, she had made herself known to Connie, lunched her, the next day. Syb told her how greatly she admired Connie's success, and Connie thanked her. Connie had not worn as well as Syb. Where Syb was still flawless, there were wrinkles on Connnie's face. But it was a mobile, intelligent, shrewd face, and Syb was honest when she said, 'I think you are splendid, Con.'

During the meal, 'Tell me one thing,' she said. 'I have always wondered. But never asked—'

'Why I could afford to go to That School?' Connie laughed.

'If what you told me was true,' Syb said, 'about those Manchester days of black pudding and tripe, how did your Pa manage the fees which were not peanuts? It took you just three days to pick up the accent. Is that what you were there for? A waste of time,' Syb said, 'considering how Northern accents swept the board, later.'

'My father was a working-class snob,' Con said. 'They don't come much more stubborn. He won a whacking prize in a sweepstake in the days when money was money. He sent me to the most expensive school he could find. I think he thought I would step right into the arms of a duke, from there. Not even a nuts and bolts heir from Brum,' Connie said.

'You didn't want a grand marriage, did you?'

'I'll tell you one thing,' Connie said. 'I wasn't fired by any driving ambition for the boards. I knew, early on, what it was like. My aunty took in theatricals. But when the time came, it was all I seemed fit for.'

'What time?'

'Dad got through the windfall.'

'All of it?'

'Helped by relatives and friends. Then he died. I told my Mum to emigrate to New Zealand with what was left. She scuttled off. And, equipped with my fine ways and my lah-di-dah accent, I started off too. And here I am. We won't go into the years between,' Connie said firmly.

'I always knew you were the best of the bunch, in school. I always knew there was more to you—'

'What are you buttering me up for?'

Syb didn't tell her. Not then.

Later, Connie was to say, 'Why are you tagging after me? What is it you want? I know you, Syb, you are after something.'

'Do you mind me tagging?'

'I've met your sort,' Connie said. When she was suspicious, as she was now, she looked like a snake. 'Women like you looking for some diversion. Too much money. Private plane. Private yacht. If it was still the days of the old railroads, a private railroad car. Just to be different. You want to be different, Syb. How?'

Then suddenly the thought struck her. 'No,' she said. 'I don't believe it. *You want to act.*'

Syb did not lack courage. She nodded.

Coldly, Connie said, 'You must be daft. You know what it is like. You are not Mrs Worthington's daughter. I told you I wouldn't talk about the years between. Short on glamour, long on disappointment,

young women spending Christmas?'

'You can't fault me there. At Cape Town,' Syb said. 'I telephoned her and invited her here. She said no, she was staying at the Cape. All planned, you see. She must want to stay. Lovely place, Cape Town,' Syb said. 'Especially at Christmas.'

You are a monster, Connie thought. Why don't you go yourself and see how things really are.

The girl is probably worth both of us put together. But she doesn't seem to get as much fun.

2

If there was a woman different from Lydia Farmer, chalk and cheese, it was Vida's sister Amalie, who was younger than Vida by twelve years. Amalie was self-confident to a degree. Diffidence she looked upon as weakness. Amalie had a bold look. Cold eyes, thin lips and an arched nose, she decided, made her look distinguished. There were times when she looked like a bird of prey.

She was a secretary to a man of business she always referred to as J.G. His importance was hers, his mantle fell upon her shoulders, she considered herself a very lucky woman to work for him. Some there were who said it might be easier to get an audience with the Pope than with J.G., if J.G.'s Miss Kettle proved obstructive.

But when it came to her private life the man in it was as different from J.G. as possible. (Did she think that when they made J.G. they broke the mould?) The man she lived with was so different from her boss that if she had deliberately searched she could not have found someone to show up the go-getting attributes of J.G.

Duke Beverley. The name was unlikely, outside the film world, but it was Duke's name. At least, he had been christened Duncan but the childish change to Duke had stuck. The Beverley was real. He was one of the kindest people one might meet, and those who knew them both wished it had been anyone but Amalie who had nabbed him.

Because she did nab him. They met at a party where Amalie did not fit in. Amalie was shrewd, yes, and smart and tried to be trendy—awful word, awful state. But there was about her no genuine wit nor intelligence. This was a party where witty people and intelligent people were thick on the ground, and Amalie should have felt lonely. She looked lonely though she was making a good pretence at enjoying herself. The intuitive, sympathetic Duke had gone over to her, introduced himself. She said, 'That is not your real name, surely?' But they went back to her flat and next day he moved in.

Duke wasn't much to look at, except for his smile. He was very tall, very thin, sandy-haired. But no one laughed at Duke or made fun except perhaps Amalie when she was fed up and had to take it out on someone. Though he himself was unaware of it, Duke had an effect on people. When you were in his company, it might happen that the flip answer, the cutting remark, died a death. The story that showed someone up for a fool didn't seem worth repeating. If he had known this, Duke would have been astonished. And embarrassed to know that there were those who cited him as one of the few really good people around.

Not that Duke was naïve or without experience of what life can get up to. He had been around. He was thirty-seven years of age. But there had remained with him something that would always be young, trusting and very kind. He acted as if malice had not yet been invented.

Of course there were those who said he put up with Amalie because of what he could get out of it in the shape of a roof above his head. For Duke seemed to have been trained for nothing and, according to Amalie, had never held down a 'proper job' in his life. 'God knows,' she had been heard to say, 'what he would do if we weren't together.' The doss house, she implied.

This was nonsense. Duke could look after himself.

You would have had to cut his heart out to find what he really thought; that he stayed because Amalie had need of him. That night at the party, the first time they met, he recognized how alone she was, and would always be, since it was not in her nature to make friends. Having excellent manners, as well as a big heart and perhaps a soft head, he never showed her what he thought, not even when she was at her worst.

She had decided they would get married, one day, if only to make Vida happy. For Vida did not care for the situation. Vida said this sort of thing was what undermined our civilization. She had said something once to Amalie about living in sin and got a reply which stopped Vida talking to her sister for all of twenty-four hours.

'But if we do marry,' Amalie told Duke, 'I expect I shall be the provider, always. I shall bring home the bacon.' Then she had relented. 'You can bring home the trivia. You know, flowers for the vases.'

Duke had acted a bit, painted a bit, but his great love was writing. Nothing serious, nothing highbrow. He liked to write short stories about what he called real people. He had had a few accepted by women's magazines, good stories, alive with warmth, humour and truth. Amalie, when she found out, poured scorn on it. 'For heaven's sake, don't let anyone find out. This isn't writing.' Her criticism had not stopped her from saying with cutting condescension, she had always believed she could write. 'If I had time—'

It had been some time now since Duke had tried to write a story. Perhaps it was because it would have to be kept secret from Amalie that stopped him. Perhaps that one thing led on to wondering how many other things he might keep secret from her, when they married, and what sort of basis was this for marriage? Usually, though, Duke lived for the day, for the present which was here with Amalie in her up-to-date flat which she adored. Duke didn't care for it. He thought it cold, with the white and grey colours she liked, and the arrangements of leaves and varnished flowers. He thought it a bit like a funeral parlour.

But he supposed she was good for him. He was someone for her to come home to. He smiled at this. It was the wrong way round.

They were to spend Christmas with Vida and Toby. 'Well, with Vida,' Amalie said. 'Toby won't do much to help. I never met a lazier man. I can't see him even attempting the job you have at the moment, Duke.'

Duke was Santa Claus at a large department store. He loved every minute of it and was perfect for it. He sat on a gold and scarlet throne in the midst of an oasis, so to speak, of artificial ice and snow, but with blue birds twittering on branches behind him and goldfish swimming in the pool near his feet. There were parrots and monkeys and reindeer. A real Christmas mish-mash. *Jingle-Bells* rang through the air as well as the sound of carols. When he described it with enthusiasm, Amalie shuddered but said she dare not come and see him. 'I should laugh so much I should spoil it for any kids there—'

'Only kids allowed,' he said proudly. 'Mas and Pas and your sort stay farther back.'

Small girls leaned in the crook of his

32

arms, shyly fingering the red stuff of his sleeves, and confessed their dreams for Christmas. Small boys, sceptical, inclined to guffaw but taking a chance, anyway, discussed Christmas man to man.

Duke loved it and them. He only wished that some of the Christmas spirit which, after all, only children possess and which adults would give their eye teeth for if the truth were known, might last beyond Christmas, over to Easter, through summer and on to next Christmas. Christmas spirit which means generosity, which means not just giving and receiving but a generosity of spirit, a giving of one's time and patience and, most of all, love.

Today, three days before the holiday, he had at this moment two clients. The morning had been hectic but now there was a lull so Duke had time to go slowly. A boy of seven or so, Duke guessed, who, from the look he had, Knew All. He knew Duke was a red-robed fake but since it was Christmas was prepared to go along. His sister, he told Duke, was three and a half. 'I had better stand close to her. She's a bit young.'

'Where is your mother?' Duke wanted to know.

'Shopping. Mrs Binns brought us here. She isn't our real aunty but we call her that. She lives in the flat above. She's good to us. Ma works, sometimes. For other people. A Daily.'

Duke nodded to show he understood. Then the boy winked at him and Duke understood this too. The wink implied that the young customer knew it was all a bit of a charade. Duke on behalf of Father Christmases everywhere, did not wink back.

He asked the girl her name.

'It's Lucy,' said the boy. 'I'm Will. Will Matthews.' He also gave the address.

'What do you want for Christmas?' Duke inquired of Lucy whose enchanting face was staring bewitched into his. But again she could not reply. Will said, 'We both want the same thing.'

'And what is that?' Duke asked.

'A good second-hand stove, and we want it now.'

There was a pause.

'Honest,' the boy said. 'That's what we want most of all. A good second-hand stove. I heard Ma say we need a new stove. There isn't a lot of money. I know that too. So I suppose it would have to be second-hand. To cook the goose in,' he explained.

Will Matthews was a sharp boy, to look at and certainly to listen to, one might well be described as bright for his age. Others might have another word for it. But one, Duke was convinced, who would consider it a waste of time 'having you on'. If Will said he wanted a stove, this was the truth. His eyes were a cold grey, bright as a ferret's eyes, Duke thought. But the mouth was wide and generous.

Duke did not ask their address. He had memorized it.

'Can you really do something about it?' Will asked.

And Duke found himself saying, 'I'll try.' The little episode stayed in his mind all afternoon.

Amalie accused him of being a romantic. He knew he was, and was unrepentant. Amalie said he was born to be conned by his belief in the goodness of human nature, and delicately she underlined the word. 'Human greed and cunning,' she lectured. 'That is what it is all about. Look out from behind your silly romantic notions,' she told him, 'at the great big world all about you, the real world of mistrust and broken promises, conceit and falsehood. This is where the truth is.'

He didn't argue. He felt sorry for her. But nothing she said changed him. He still tried to see the best in most things.

After work, he looked up the street where the children said they lived, and took a bus there.

An ordinary London street, one of thousands. Long and grey like paper houses cut into a chain, each house at one time the home of a single family but flats now, each house thus doing duty for four or more houses. No gardens. Front steps leading to a porch, an area beneath. And not a tree in sight.

Duke read the cards slotted in beside the front door. *Mrs C. Matthews.*

He entered, found the appropriate door, rang the bell.

The young woman who opened the door to him was pretty, with brown hair and Will's grey eyes but not as cold as Will's eyes. She smiled and greeted him but looked astonished, as well she might, when Duke said, 'It's occurred to me—will she recognize me? Lucy. Will she recognize me as Santa Claus? I met them today.'

She said she didn't think Lucy would

know him. Not without the beard.

'Does she still believe?' Duke asked. 'It isn't a question I could ask at the time.'

'I'm not certain. They are cagey, aren't they? Will knows—'

'Of course. He asked me something, this morning—' Duke said. She invited him in. She knew as well as anyone that these days it was only prudent to demand credentials before you did this but told herself she trusted this man on sight. And it would be a dyed-in-the-wool villain who took in vain the name of Santa Claus to commit a crime. 'I am Cherry Matthews,' she told him. When he said, 'Duke Beverley', she didn't turn a hair.

Cherry Matthews had spent the first fifteen years of her life in Wales and had never forgotten, nor tried to, the traditional Welsh greeting. 'How are you? Come in. Have a cup of tea.'

The room was small and seemed to Duke, used to Amalie's cunningly contrived spacing, cosily over full of furniture. But it was a warm, happy place. He sensed it and felt at home at once. Will, who was reading at the table, looked up and grinned. 'Thought you would come,' he said.

'I hope,' said his mother, 'you didn't worry this gentleman.'

'Just told him we had a problem,' Will said.

Over tea, Cherry told her visitor something of her story. Bert Matthews had died two years ago. 'We had a house but I sold it and came here. There's a bit of money,' Cherry admitted. 'I go out sometimes as a Daily. Sometimes I take Lucy or she stays with a neighbour. People are very kind. Don't you believe it when they call London an unfriendly place.'

Duke didn't. He found it friendly too.

But it wasn't just other people with Cherry Matthews. Friendly herself, outgiving, she made most people respond in kind. When Bert died, she tried to hide her grief and make certain the children missed nothing. They had lived in Kent, she said. She was an orphan and Bert only had an aunt. So Cherry had moved to London to be near the aunt. 'Six months later, she emigrated to Canada. Still, she's happy there.'

It was important to Cherry that people be allowed to do what they wanted to do and be happy. When Duke told her about the request for the second-hand stove, her eyes misted. 'Bless them. It's Absalom, you see.'

Duke shook his head. He stretched his long legs towards the fire and settled down to hear the story. By this time Lucy was in bed and Will on the way, but slowly. Duke and Cherry chatted like old friends.

'Absalom. The old goose. Bert had a friend who is a farmer. We spent a week there in the summer and he showed us the goose he said he was giving us for Christmas. He said he looked on the geese as his sons, so we christened it Absalom. Lucy calls it Abby so it seems almost cannibalistic to eat it. But not quite,' she admitted frankly. 'I'm grateful. Other Christmases, we have had a chicken. The goose won't go into my stove.'

'Where I lived,' Duke reminisced, 'in the country, a small town, some people— rented out, would you say?—space in the ovens of the local bakehouses for cooking their Christmas bird. Those with ovens like yours and too-big geese. I used to watch them bringing the dinner home. We lived in a house on the main street.' (A Regency gem of a house, but Duke didn't say so.) 'My mother was not only punctual for everything. She was far too

early for most things. When she marched
us off to church service, the neighbours
knew it was time they might leisurely
get ready. So our Christmas dinner was
finished by twelve-thirty. Then I would sit
at the window and watch the people scurry
on home carrying a big pan covered with
a snow white cloth, under it the cooked
goose or turkey.'

'Like something out of Dickens.'

'I always thought so.'

Will, in striped pyjamas, came to say
good night, and to tell Duke, 'I thought
you would do something. I reckoned you
have that sort of face.'

A con? Duke preferred to think the word
was *trusting*. But he was glad, whatever it
was, his face had appealed to Will.

'But do you know where you can get
one?' Will said, the ferrety look much in
evidence.

'I'll do my best. I can't say yes, right
out. But I'll try.'

'Good enough.' Evidently Duke's honesty
had won again. Will held out his hand.
Duke shook it. 'Sealing a bargain,' Will
said. If so, he was getting the best of it.
Naturally.

It was eight o'clock when Duke left.

Cherry didn't know when she had enjoyed an evening more.

Perhaps fortunately, Amalie was at a staff party at which function she was not thinking of Duke. She was trying to keep as close as she could to any one of the directors.

'I'll be back tomorrow,' Duke told Cherry. 'With some news, I hope.'

She told him how much she was able to give for the stove. Seriously, he nodded. Amalie would have been surprised at such seriousness. One of her many accusations against him was that he didn't seem to know the value of money.

But Duke was unlucky. He telephoned a few friends who were surprised at his request and had to say no, they were not thinking of getting rid of their stoves, not now, not with Christmas so near.

3

On Christmas Eve afternoon Duke and Amalie were to drive into the country to Vida's where they would spend the holiday. The store, and Santa Claus, packed up at mid-day, Amalie grumbled at having to leave London so late in the day. She said she never cared to be one of a mob and everyone, but everyone, would be in their cars then. 'I don't mean our sort,' she told Duke snobbishly. 'People like J.G. and the rest of the directors went yesterday. All the little proles in their little cars, dashing about. I can't bear it. There are to be no more Christmases to be spoiled like this,' she ordered him. And in case he didn't understand, 'No more of this Santa Claus farce.'

'You go early,' he told her. 'Go right after breakfast. I'll follow later.'

She considered this, then said, 'I'll tell you one thing. If you are not here by two o'clock, not one minute later, I shall go off on my own. You can follow what time you like.'

43

But that night, the eve of Christmas Eve, Duke had an idea. It was so simple and so perfect he wondered why he had not thought of it before. Of course, he had to keep it secret from Amalie, at least now, before she left. He knew she would not agree but if it came out later, it would be over, the deed done. Quite literally, the goose cooked.

If he and Amalie were away from the flat for Christmas, why couldn't Cherry cook Absalom here? Nothing would happen to spoil Amalie's kitchen. You only had to see Cherry's little home to realize what sort of a housekeeper she was. Christmas was the time for helping one another. If it had a message, he thought, surely this was it. As he lay awake, savouring the plan, into Duke's mind came a procession of little figures happily bearing home from the bakehouse the Christmas bird.

It did not occur to him that, the flat being Amalie's she would say he had no right to offer the use of it to anyone. If the flat were his, and a friend of hers was in a fix for the want of a stove, Duke would not have thought twice about lending the kitchen.

I suppose I am bound to tell her, he

thought, after Christmas. I am bound to blurt it out. But it will be over, then. Will won't be disappointed. It was important, this. And not only not disappointed in Duke at not being able to fix things. Disappointed in his looked-forward-to Christmas dinner.

When he left for his last day at the store, Amalie said, 'Remember. If you are not here by two o'clock, I shall go without you.'

'Yes.'

'What do you mean—yes?'

'Yes, I understand,' he said.

'What I am threatening?'

He laughed. 'All right. If that's what you are doing.'

She told him he never took anything seriously. 'And you didn't get your hair cut as you promised. Vida will comment. It's hanging over your collar.'

'Like most men in London.'

'Theirs is properly shaped.'

He laughed again and came into the bedroom and leaned over the bed and kissed her. 'Oh, you—' she said but had to smile back at him. It was pleasant, most times, having Duke around. She had bought him an expensive cashmere sweater for Christmas in a shade she particularly liked.

Being Duke, he thought he would have time, after work, to call at the Matthews flat, sell his plan to Cherry, then be back in time to drive with Amalie to Vida's.

Being Duke, it didn't work. Being Duke, people had a way of snarling up his plans, his affection for them and his care that things went right for them.

Will said immediately, opening the door himself. 'Where is it?'

'Will—' Cherry sounded cross and she was cross. She was sorry Will had told Duke about the stove. Not sorry she had met him, not that. But Will was hounding him and he was sensitive, Cherry knew that he was, and he might be hurt and she didn't want him to be. Already, she felt protective towards him. She believed that however much he tried to hide it, he was easily hurt and had been hurt, many times, but as often as it happened, he forgave.

How old is he? Nearly forty, I should think. He will never get on, not the way people expect, these days, and try for. He will let others push him around, he will stand aside while they nip on, he won't do

46

anything like tripping them up or elbowing them out of the way.

He really is a lovely person. And his voice. I could listen to it for ever. He has a lovely voice.

When they were inside, Will could contain himself no longer. 'You have let us down.' He looked like one of the Mafia, junior branch.

'Stop that,' his mother repeated. 'We can manage.'

'How?' Will demanded.

Lucy nestled in Duke's arms. She treated him to *Mary, Mary, Quite Contrary*. He listened with all his attention. He told Will, 'I've thought of something. I suggest you cook Absalom in my flat. There will be no one there. Amalie and I are to spend Christmas in the country.'

And for the moment the world darkened for Cherry. Of course he had told her about Amalie, but Cherry had had a crazy thought he was asking her to cook dinner for four, himself included.

'Is your stove big enough?' he heard Will ask. 'You should see that goose. He's in the scullery on the table. I don't think any old stove will do. I think the Queen's stove would be just about right. I think—'

47

'*Quiet,*' his mother said. 'You think too much.'

'Think before you speak,' Lucy crooned, lapsing into fat chuckles at her own wit.

Will looked at her beadily, then smiled too. Duke could have died for them both. He really loved them.

Absalom was indeed a whopper among geese. Calm, cold, plucked, he lay on a huge platter and still some of him was over the edge. 'There's a goose for you,' Will said admiringly.

'I mean what I said about the stove in our flat,' Duke told Cherry.

'Thank you. But I couldn't. Not in a strange kitchen. Some women might but I couldn't.'

Yes, he thought, some women might. If J.G. offered Amalie Kettle the use of his kitchen, she would be there like a shot.

They stood looking at one another.

Cherry thought, 'My God, I hope she is good to him because I've got a suspicion she isn't good for him. She has a good man there. I hope she knows it.'

And Duke was thinking of Cherry's Christmas, this year again, without Bert. She had never said a word, not once, about being lonely. He was certain she was. He smiled. 'Right,' he said happily. 'I shall stay there with you tomorrow morning while you cook it. I'll fetch you and I'll stay with you.' He suddenly felt extremely happy.

'You were going away,' Cherry reminded him but she was smiling.

'I'll go there later in the day.'

'They will miss you,' she said. He shrugged.

'You will miss your Christmas dinner there,' she said. He told her they had it in the evening. 'Oh, yes,' she said. She didn't care when they had it. She was going to have the joy of his company all tomorrow morning.

He said gently, 'Don't fuss. Say yes.' A strange thing, he, who never planned anything—it was a joke with Amalie that Duke could not run his own life let alone anyone else's, meaning hers—seemed to know just the right thing for this young woman and her family.

'Thank you,' she said. 'I'll come, and I'm grateful. It will be quite an adventure. Would you like a cup of tea? I'm sorry. I should have asked you—'

Duke said calmly, 'And a sandwich if you have something—'

'O-oh,' her dismay was comical. 'I didn't know you were hungry. Sit down. I have some nice ham. Fresh bread.' So Duke sat, Lucy on his knees, while Cherry made him ham sandwiches and brewed fresh tea. 'Ambrosia,' Duke said it was, which word had to be explained to Will who thereupon got out pencil and paper and made a list of what to him was ambrosia. Fish and chips headed the list. After the sandwiches, Duke raided the fruit bowl. Happily Cherry watched him. Sometimes she thought he was like a third child in her family. When Duke remarked on the apples, Will said, 'From the stall in the Market. The man there is keen on Ma.'

'Will—' Cherry gasped.

'Shows he has eyes in his head and uses them,' Duke calmly agreed. He winked at Will who winked back. Duke looked at the clock. He had forgotten to think of Amalie at two o'clock. It was a bit late now. It was four-thirty. He said, 'Why not come round now and see the flat? Then it won't spring such a surprise, tomorrow morning. If there is anything you need which isn't there, you will know to bring it.'

'Your young lady—?' Cherry began.

'She left early,' Duke said.

So they went round to the flat in a taxi. It made Will Matthews feel wonderfully rich, riding in a taxi. He didn't say anything but stared out of the window at the Christmas crowds, pitying them for having to walk. Lucy sat on Duke's knee, and the driver, if he thought of it at all, probably thought them a nice little Christmas family, up to see the lights. He wished them a Merry Christmas when they got out.

Cherry was determined not to be overawed by the place. She wasn't. She thought it looked a bit anaemic, all those cold colours. It was, too, a woman's room. Where did Duke fit in? If he wanted to sprawl in a chair, watching Match of the Day, was he allowed to?

The kitchen, bright blue and gleaming white, with touches of terracotta, was straight off the glossy pages. Like its mistress, she thought.

What's the matter with you? You've never met her, yet you condemn her, out of hand?

I don't have to meet her. He doesn't seem happy. He could be happy. It's a treat to see him smile.

51

Why doesn't she marry him? He's a catch.

She did not want to come here to cook. The idea was absurd. But she knew she would have tried to cook Absalom over a tinker's fire if this man suggested she did. When all this was over and he disappeared out of their lives, he would take some forgetting. She wished she did not have to contemplate forgetting him.

If his mother made a good show of enthusiasm, Will was enchanted with everything. One day, he would give his mother and Lucy a kitchen like this. But to be honest it would be the giving that would count with Will. There were no illusions about who came first in his world.

The telephone rang, Duke excused himself and went in to the bedroom to answer it.

'Where are you?' Amalie demanded. 'I did what I said I would do. I left at five minutes past two. The traffic was awful. What happened?'

'I met some chaps I knew. We went to a pub.'

'A fine thing for Santa Claus to do—'

'If anyone needs a drink, he does.'

'What friends?' Amalie demanded to be told.

'Chaps I was at Oxford with.' And for once he said it deliberately for this was one of the things that counted with her. A reference to his Oxford days. She was proud of them and mentioned them herself more than he did which wasn't difficult because he never talked about them. She also harangued him for not having made more use of them and of the people he had met there. She said, 'Now I suppose you are in no state to drive here tonight?'

'That's true.' He thought how shamefully easy it is to lie on the telephone, and he smiled, thinking it. He told her he would be there early the next day.

He gave Cherry a drink in the sitting-room, and the children an orange drink. He sadly noticed Cherry sat on the edge of the chair.

'You have no paper chains,' Lucy said. 'No Christmas Tree.' Her lids drooped as if she could weep for him.

He explained that he had not meant to spend Christmas here. 'Will there be a Tree where you are going?' she asked. When he said yes, she went on, 'And paper chains?'

53

'Well, not paper chains. But great bunches of holly and mistletoe and evergreens. And a wreath on the front door of evergreens and red ribbons.'

Lucy was satisfied that he was not going to be underprivileged.

'I'll just look at the kitchen again,' Will said. 'If Absalom could come back to life, for an instant, and see it, he would think it just the job.'

He went off with Lucy trotting behind.

Duke said gently. 'If you could think it is just the job, if you could accept, you will have made my Christmas, Cherry,'

For him, she made the effort. She said, 'Of course. It's kind of you. But you will stay to Christmas dinner? If they have theirs in the evening—'

'By Jove, yes. Two Christmas dinners in one day. I've never had that before.'

'You can do with it,' she said, forthrightly. 'You are skinny enough.'

When they were at home again, Will and Lucy and their mother, Will addressed Absalom. 'You should see the place! Fit for a king,' Will said. 'What a way to go—' he told the goose, kindly. Then, 'Ma? We'll take the crackers, eh?'

'Yes.'

'Ma?'

'What?'

'What about his presents?'

'Will!' Cherry clapped her hand over her mouth, stared at him in horror.

Not for the first time, Will Matthews was head of the house. He said the stalls were still open in the Market.

She bundled Lucy back into her warm clothes and took them both out with her. They were in Paradise with the darkness cut with diamond bright lights, the crowds, the noise, the stalls. Christmas all around. She bought a scarf in brown wool as her present to Duke and a pair of gloves, the same colour, from the children. 'That shirt would be better than dull old gloves,' Will said, pointing to a gleaming white shirt, frilled, at the front of the stall. 'We don't know him well enough to buy him a shirt,' Cherry said. Then, to cheer herself up, said, 'Perhaps next year.'

Next morning, Duke called for them. Children, parcels, goose, mother, all were piled in. It was a tight squeeze but it was Christmas incarnate. While Cherry prepared the dinner, Will and Lucy played with their presents in the hallway of the flat. Will said it was better there. The carpet was darker if anything should go wrong.

'Nothing is to go wrong,' his mother ordered.

Nothing did.

Duke gave Will and Lucy a gift of money. To Cherry he gave a brooch which had belonged to his mother, seed pearls in a setting of gold, a small thing which he had treasured for years. At first he had meant to give it to Amalie but the time was never the right time. He had known for years he would never give it to her. She might accept it but she would put it away and never wear it. Cherry was overwhelmed. Her eyes were bright with tears as she thanked him. She didn't spoil it by telling him he should not have done it. She pinned it on to her dress. 'I shall wear it always,' she said simply, and he was glad to hear her say it. 'Do that,' he said. 'It's had a disappointing life stuck away in a box in a drawer.' And he sat in the kitchen while she cooked, talking about his mother and his father and his early life, about school and about Oxford. Cherry drank in what he was saying.

The meal, in Will's opinion, was fit for the Queen. Roast goose with stuffing.

Apple sauce. Roast potatoes and peas. Gravy. Cherry's home-made pudding with the silver trinkets cunningly hidden. Mince pies. The children found room for a helping of everything. Will wore an admiral's paper hat, Lucy a crown. Cherry's hat was a yellow sunflower. Duke wore a bonnet. He drank nothing because he was driving up to Vida's. 'But I'll call in in the New Year and celebrate with you then.'

So the world brightened again for her, in the way it kept bright and shadowed when she thought she might or might not see him. Then she said, 'Trust me to tidy up—I shall leave everything as I found it—then you can start off for the country right away.'

'Not right away after a meal this size,' he said contentedly. 'We'll drink our coffee in the sitting-room. I'll help you wash up. I'll see you home.'

'No—'

'Yes,' he gently corrected. So she smiled, scooped the sleepy Lucy in her arms and carried her in to the bedroom to rest. Will returned to the hallway where he had left a gory battle, half won or lost, depending whose side Will was on. When Cherry returned to the sitting-room, Duke put his arms round her and kissed her on the mouth. 'A Merry Christmas.'

'Oh, it is.' She wanted to cling to him and say, 'You did mean it when you said you will come and see us in the New Year? On New Year's Day? It isn't going to end with you seeing us home, me closing the door, and thinking it was all a fairy tale—'

He seemed to know what she was thinking. He said, 'It's no fairy tale, what has happened. There is Absalom's carcase to prove it.'

So she blinked away the tears and laughed instead.

When they were ready to leave, she said, 'Will you tell your young lady?'

'I expect so. I don't see how I can keep it to myself, the nicest thing that has happened in years.'

'Then will you give her this?' Cherry turned to get the handsome cyclamen she had hidden up to then. 'To say thank you.'

Duke was genuinely delighted. 'I wondered what was in that green paper.' They put the plant in a dark green pot which Cherry said was just the thing.

He took the family home, saw them safely in, and left.

For the kids' sake, she told herself, she must make the effort. She did. They played games and they sang songs. Will sang solos. Lucy made up humming songs which they gravely listened to and applauded. Cherry read to Lucy. Will was allowed to stay up an extra hour. They had had a good Christmas, in Will's opinion. But he was shocked that he could eat so little supper. Just a glass of milk and biscuit. He went to take one last look at the goose. Plenty there for tomorrow.

Lydia Farmer would have been happy to take part in Cherry Matthew's Christmas. It would have been Christmas as Lydia thought it should be kept. An intimate family celebration. Small children for good measure.

There was a dance at the hotel. And the meal was sumptuous, there was no other word. She joined a party at the invitation of the friendly dowager who organized it. She dressed, as she herself described it, to kill, because tonight competition would be fierce. But when she let slip at the table that she would be back in England very soon there was a howl of disbelief. They said she was mad. England was spring, summer or autumn. Never winter. England was strawberries and cream and roses round the door. England was Wimbledon in June. England was Henley and Cowes. England was the Season, a visit for a round of theatres and shops. But England in January? Not to be thought of.

I shall be going home, she had persisted, smiling.

They hoped her home had central heating.

Lydia had written Toby to tell him she was coming. Not to ask if she might come. She told him. She would be welcome, she thought, of course she would. She would be part of the family.

4

Vida Farmer said she loved Christmas, that it was the season with the greatest hold on her heart. She was fond of saying woolly things like this. Certainly, she made her preparations for Christmas. Cakes, puddings, mince pies, enough for an orphanage. She said she wished the house could hold more than her immediate family for so wonderful a holiday, many more. She wished she might fill it with lonely people. There was nothing to stop her, except that she didn't mean a word of what she said.

Toby put up with Christmas, enjoying the food and drink. Each year, Syb sent a hamper of food which, addressed to Mr and Mrs Farmer, everyone knew was for Toby. Vida tried not to eat any of the contents. Carlsbad plums. A Stilton cheese. Peaches in syrup. Handmade chocolates. Vida would tick the items off disapprovingly and say, 'It seems terrible to pay such a price for a hamper of food. This must have cost a hundred pounds, Toby. People are hard up—starving—'

Toby, unpacking the hamper, did not listen to her.

'My little short crust mincepies,' Vida grizzled. 'My cake iced with the robins on it and the yule log. Not much, I suppose, compared with this. But at least my things were made with love. I haven't asked a shop to send a hamper, impersonally. I think this is the worst sort of present. It means nothing.'

Perhaps it is stupid for me to get worked up but I cannot stand her! She is vulgar. Rich and vulgar. I don't believe in revolutions because people like us could lose so much. But I wouldn't mind seeing *her* lose her money. If she had to work it would stop her sending hampers to people who are never really hungry anyway. Toby has three meals a day, and always has had. One thing, though, she doesn't get anything from Toby, at Christmas or at any time. That's something his laziness is responsible for, thank God. Aloud, she said, 'This should have gone to an orphanage—'

'The orphans wouldn't appreciate the Stilton,' Toby said. Then he said Syb

62

donated a lot to charity. 'More than we do.'

'She has more to give. I give what I can. There isn't a charity envelope pushed through the door I don't examine. Of course, some appeal to me more than others. But donations are easy when you are as rich as she is.'

But she knew Toby wasn't listening. He was reading the label on a tin of exotic soup. Vida flounced out to look for Ben. She had ordered him to start cutting evergreens in the garden ready for decorations. He was.

Ben, in his mid-seventies, was more than twenty years Vida's senior. He was a handsome old man. Tall, thin, white-haired, blue-eyed. My *verray parfit gentil knight,* Vida called him. Nobody argued.

It was a strange little story, one you might not associate with practical, bustling Vida. Ben had known her when she was young and had always been fond of her. Perhaps it was her good housekeeping that appealed to him. Ben was fond of the quiet, ordered life. Here he resembled Toby except that Toby would never move from where he was comfortable while Ben might move on, if the chance arose, to a cushier billet. Toby recognized this. Vida did not. She thought herself Lady Bountiful, the giver of good things to Ben now in the evening of his days. She could not imagine him anywhere else. 'Little Vida,' he called her. He said she was like a little squirrel. Maybe this wasn't a bad description. Running hither and yon, searching for food, foraging, storing, taking a nip and a bite at anything that delayed or frustrated. Not an attractive beast, despite the bushy tail.

Vida had kept in touch with Ben (his admiration had always pleased her) and when, some years before, she heard he was living alone, went in search of him and, brooking no argument (he gave none) took him back with her to live with Toby and herself. Ben had been ill and recuperated there. Recovery complete, Ben stayed on. He was part of the family, Vida always said, a fixture.

'Of course,' she confided to her nearest friends, 'Ben pays *a small amount* to stay with us. A laughable sum, derisory. But I am of the opinion it is better to contribute something, however small, better for host and guest. It gives independence to the guest and satisfaction to the other side. Of course, Ben would not get elsewhere the attention he gets with us. Not for the mite he contributes. But that is what friendship is for. To help in times of need.'

'Let him stay,' Toby had said. 'But for God's sake don't ask the old chap to pay anything.' So Ben's mite was a secret between him and Vida and Vida's friends, none of whom were likely to tell Toby because when they were around he made himself scarce.

The same friends told Vida they thought Ben Bartlow looked like a retired diplomat or like the man in any expensive advertisement. He looked distinguished, they said. Or like a writer, a poet. The funny thing about Vida, one of them, was that she never liked nice things to be said about other people, not even about her friends. It irritated her, in some way, that they were being praised and not she. So when people said he looked like a poet, she would laugh and say, 'Ben never writes a letter if he can help it. Too much trouble to put pen to paper. I tell him I suspect he can't spell and is ashamed to let it be known!'

Perhaps. But what Ben was was an excellent raconteur. It is a delightful accomplishment, when not done to excess, but one that seems to be out of favour now. Ben remembered vividly his life as a boy and an old man. Sometimes Toby listened when he reminisced. Not Vida. She said she had no time.

'He comes from a good family,' she would say, to any friend who inquired, and she made it sound like a reference. 'A manor house, I believe. Two brothers killed in World War One. The father drank himself to death. The mother broke her neck in the hunting field. These people are careless, aren't they? The house was sold long ago. He has nowhere to go. We don't talk about it. Better to forget, I say.'

Now, in the garden, among the evergreens, Vida grumbled to Ben about the hamper which had arrived. Ben told her not to let it annoy her. 'You know everything is over between them.'

'I should hope so.' Then Vida went off on another tack. 'I wish Duke would give Amalie a ring for Christmas. It would be the best present he could give her.'

Ben looked puzzled. 'A ring?' He couldn't think what sort of ring Amalie might want.

'I wish they would marry. I may be old-fashioned,' Vida said, 'but this living together is, in my opinion, flying in the face of Holy Writ.'

Ben wondered fleetingly what Vida would have done if Toby Farmer had suggested they live in sin. She would no doubt have said, 'Blow Holy Writ—'

Tben Vida went on to grumble, as she had so often before, that Amalie was not the woman for such as Duke. 'She should marry a business man. Plenty where she is. That man will be a brake on her. She doesn't take him anywhere, now.'

Not that Vida really cared much for career women. She said a woman's place was in the home and that she thought the Lord was unfair to Martha.

She hoped Ellie thought the same. She had never asked her. But it was plain that Ellie was no career woman. Vida said she didn't mind what Ellie did in her job, what mattered was that Ellie marry happily and live near enough to Vida for Vida to enjoy her grandchildren.

'I think I shall have deserved a happy old age, after a lifetime spent making others happy.'

Vida thought it a shame when children

67

married and went to live away from home, far away. If Ellie ever said she was going to, say, New Zealand to live with her husband, Vida admitted that she herself might not behave well, if this is what it is called. She would cry, kick up a fuss, make Ellie try to see where her duty lay, especially as an only child, a daughter. Ellie's duty would be to stay near home. After all, Vida would be such a help to her. Think of everything she could tell her from making meringues to bringing up baby.

Not that she thought Ellie would leave. A real home girl, Ellie. Why, she hadn't been happy at boarding school.

No, no greener grass for Ellie. Ellie must marry a professional man, a solicitor or an architect or a school master, and settle down near Wadden. Vida and Ellie would have fun choosing things for Ellie's new home. Young bride, the new recruit. Seasoned campaigner, the mother.

Vida did not know many of Ellie's friends, the young people she went around with, but she told herself she would know at once when there was Someone Special. She won't be able to hide it from me, not from her mother. Then we can start planning the wedding. This is a charming place to hold a reception in. Toby and Ellie will look lovely walking down the aisle. I shall wear blue. Blue-eyed women should always wear blue.

So perhaps it was as well Vida did not know who Ellie's friends were. Ellie was a practised liar and adept at pulling the wool over her mother's eyes. And Ellie had just one ambition which was to get away from home as soon as possible, to go to London to work and to live what, in Ellie's words, was the good life. She didn't know how she would attain all this but she wouldn't give up trying. By golly, no. In the meantime Ellie did as little work in her job as she could get away with and played as hard after work as Wadden allowed.

To look at, Ellie was not exciting. Brown hair, hazel eyes. Her teeth were her best asset but since she was usually sulky they did not redeem her much. She persisted in wearing her hair straight and long which made her father cry, 'For God's sake, tie your hair back. You look like a mad woman.' This didn't help the sulks.

Ellie worked in an office and was ambivalent about it, sometimes looking down on the other girls, sometimes going around with them because there was no one else.

Indeed, Vida would not have approved of some of them. Their language and their behaviour would rightly have shocked her. But to Ellie they made up for the dullness at home. She herself was gaining quite a reputation among them for wildness. The other girls did not like her, they didn't trust her. But they were all of an age and that was the thing that bound them together. Their age against authority. Ellie understood this.

She had vowed this was the last boring old Christmas she would spend at home. Next year she would be in London, and you wouldn't see her on Christmas Eve one of the crowd on the railway station making for home. Not Ellie. Once away, they could whistle for her.

But how to take the first step towards this longed-for freedom? Her father wouldn't help. He had paid for her to go to an expensive boarding school. Vida had insisted he did. 'Lydia got the best Syb could give her. So will Ellie,' Vida firmly said. When Ellie left without a blushing honour near her, Toby said in effect, 'Right. You've had your whack. Now go on from here.' When Ellie muttered she had to train for something, he said there was a secretarial college in Wadden. It was near the golf club. He had noticed the board outside when he motored to the club. He told her to go there. Her mother could pay the fees out of the housekeeping money. 'What if I had been clever?' Ellie had flared. 'What would you have done?'

Toby told her this was a hypothetical question, and told her to look the word up.

If there was anyone Ellie envied, it was Lydia, her half-sister. Lydia's freedom, her money. Lydia, Ellie marvelled, was an heiress, no less. And Lydia didn't live with her mother. Lydia went where she liked. One of the Beautiful People, Lydia. Almost. She wondered if Lydia might not help her get away. If they met, she could put her case to Lydia. But where were they going to meet? Lydia was never in England. Lucky devil.

But whenever she mentioned Lydia to her mother the reaction was the same. Vida showed visible signs of annoyance. Her round little face turned from rosy plum to wrinkled prune, thought Vida's loving daughter. Ellie got some inkling of what was wrong when, purely from mischief, she one day asked Vida what they would do if Lydia wanted the house back.

'What do you mean, want it back?' Vida flared. 'Why should she want it? It isn't her home.'

'It's her property,' Ellie said. 'And she was born here. What if she suddenly becomes sentimental about the place?' the wickedly teasing Ellie continued. 'People do. They get tired of travelling. What if she marries and decides nothing but this house will do?'

'She can't turn us out. If she wants a place, there is the house on the hill.'

'The Ellworthys don't give her any trouble. Model tenants,' Ellie said. 'Why should she turn them out? They pay rent. We get this free.'

Vida had told her to be quiet, not to keep on about something that would never happen. But you do think about it, Ellie chuckled to herself. One of the thoughts that nest on the pillow beside you on a sleepless night. *What if the day ever comes when Lydia wants this place?*

Ellie was right. It was Vida's secret fear, almost dread, they might be turned out of the house. She loved it so much. To have to leave would be a kind of death to her and she knew it. She could not imagine herself living elsewhere. How her friends would laugh, she knew they would, to see her turned out when she had always made it plain she thought herself the luckiest of women to live here. Houses were expensive today. She and Toby could not afford to buy another house like this. Not that Toby would bother to look. He wouldn't mind where they lived as long as it was near a golf course.

Lydia won't come back. What is there for her here?

She might come back. As Ellie said, she might marry and want to live here as her mother did. Toby would leave if Lydia asked him to. If Lydia found another house for us I should hate it from the first day.

Fear was a viper in Vida's bosom, and to know that the same thought had occurred to Ellie made the fear more real and therefore sharper. The times when she forgot about it grew less. It came close to an obsession.

When Amalie arrived, the outward appearance of the house pleased her. The lights gleamed, there was a splendid view of the Christmas Tree in the sitting-room strategically placed so that visitors had a good view. A holly wreath was attached to the front door by red ribbons. It looked a picture and Amalie liked things to look like this. In her world there was no room for spontaneity or impromptu decisions. She distrusted both. Life was for living by rules, her rules. She knew that she herself, in suede coat with fur collar and fur hat, fitted into the picture. *Guest arriving for Christmas*. Like a glossy page from a Sunday supplement.

'Where is Duke?' Vida asked, peering out from the porch. When Amalie explained, Vida said, 'Serves him right.' She thought him a gormless creature. Fancy not getting back in time to motor here with Amalie. It is rude to me, as his hostess. In addition to the fact that he and her sister were not married, there were other things about Duke which annoyed Vida. That voice. It was almost as if Vida thought he had no right to it but even she could not go so far as to think it affected. Even his good easy manners annoyed Vida. Penniless, she thought. Almost a lay-about.

When Amalie telephoned later to find out what had happened to Duke, she came back to tell Vida he would arrive next day. 'He will miss a good supper this evening,' Vida said.

Ellie felt sorry for Duke. At this moment, Amalie's face and Vida's looked almost alike in cold disapproval. If Duke did marry Amalie, Ellie thought he was in for a thin time. Ellie did not like her aunt. Amalie criticized Ellie's clothes, her attitude towards what Amalie called her future, even my face, Ellie brooded. If Amalie is due to stay, I can be certain of a spot on my chin. And will she remark on it? Of course she will. The only thing Ellie liked about Amalie was her wardrobe. Amalie looked good tonight in sand-coloured jersey and skirt, expensive high boots, row upon row of beads round her neck. Will she give me just one chain? Will she heck!

The letter from Lydia to Toby telling him she was coming home to spend some time with them arrived with the last stragglers of mail on Christmas morning, and for once it was Toby who picked up the envelopes from the hall table. He recognized Lydia's writing on the air letter and slipped it into his pocket to read later.

Vida, when she saw the mail, pounced on the Christmas cards, sighed with genuine relief that she was not in what would be to her the awful, shameful predicament of receiving a card from someone to whom she had not sent one. She boasted with truth it never happened.

Vida much enjoyed church service on Christmas morning, and even with Duke absent she thought they put up a good show. An English family. She smiled as she thought it. Toby, herself and Ellie. Amalie. Ben. She was glad Duke wasn't there. She always felt a little ashamed of him. His height and the carroty brightness of his hair, his beak of a nose. She had said it before and she would say it now. She simply did not know what Amalie saw in him. And that checked coat he wore, flapping round him like a tent. And a scarf wound round his neck. He always looked as if he was going to watch a Rugby match.

She sang the hymns with gusto. She had a pretty voice. Toby and Ben sang as well. Amalie sang when she felt like it. Ellie kept silent.

They shook hands with the vicar in the porch and wished him a Merry Christmas, and Vida thought again how English it all was, and thought of the Royal family at Windsor.

There was a buffet lunch. Then the presents were handed out by Vida. 'Shouldn't we wait for Duke?' Ellie said mischievously. 'Shouldn't we wait until he comes before handing out the presents?'

'Certainly not,' Vida snapped. 'We don't wait for anyone. There are only two presents for him anyway.'

'He has sent one to each of us,' Ellie said. Vida thought, though she just didn't say it, that Amalie had probably bought the presents.

At dinner time, Duke was still absent. 'Telephone the police,' Ellie said. When Amalie told her not to be absurd, Ellie went on, 'The alternative to you being stood up is that there has been an accident.' Amalie told her to shut up.

When he had returned to the flat after seeing Cherry and her family safely home, Duke had taken a nap. Perhaps he should not have returned to the flat but he had forgotten toothbrush and pyjamas. He sat for a moment in an armchair. This was fatal. When he awoke and saw the time he was horrified. He drove as fast as he could to where retribution awaited.

On Christmas afternoon, Toby and Ben slept. Amalie disappeared to her room. Ellie said she was going for a walk. 'Where? Who with?' Vida asked. 'On my own,' Ellie lied. 'Just a walk.'

Alone in the kitchen, Vida prepared the evening meal. She was one of those who, refusing help, yet grumble when they go it alone. Every year, she told herself, it is the same. I am expected to do everything. And what thanks do I get?

Ellie met in the village the boy she had planned to meet. He took her for what he described as a spin to the coast in his new sports car. Then he drove her back to where they had met, and Ellie walked home. This little episode made her day, as she told herself. Nothing pleased her more than pulling the wool over adult eyes. My mother would have a fit if she knew the half I do. She would never believe Johnny and I had been to the coast and back. 'You couldn't have done it in the time,' Vida would say. Well, we did. Johnny wanted to show off. He put his foot down and we got there in record time. Vida didn't care for Johnny whose father was a bookmaker. Ellie didn't care what Johnny's father was. It was the car that mattered.

But when it came to decorating the dinner table, Amalie did her bit. The motif was gold and silver sophistication. Cute-faced angels, fat cherubs, stars and tiny trees of gold and silver. All very charming and a long way from Christmas.

Amalie had bought crackers, also gilt and silver. She said they looked so perfect it was a shame to pull them. 'Then leave them for next year,' Toby said. Amalie looked sharply at him.

The meal was perfection. Amalie got the coin in her piece of the pudding and Ellie the ring. 'Quite right,' Vida said. 'You, Amalie, will get a rise in pay. Ellie will be married soon.' Ellie choked on her pudding.

'Amalie could do with hearing the old Wedding March,' Toby said. He did not like Amalie and did like teasing her, especially now against what he thought was a phoney background of goodwill.

'My heavens,' Vida said. 'Duke. Amalie, I forgot about him. Where is he?'

'I telephoned the flat just before dinner,' her sister told her. 'There was no reply. He is probably on the way here.'

As if on cue the doorbell rang.

It was Duke. To add to his lateness, the car had broken down. When he apologized to Vida, as he should since she was his hostess, she told him it was Amalie he should apologize to. Amalie only turned her cheek for him to kiss, a cold pale cheek which cooled the kiss.

Toby greeted Duke cheerfully. He liked him and only hoped something would intervene to stop Amalie marrying him. While Duke went to take off his coat and scarf and to freshen up, as Vida put it, Toby carved a monster plate of ham and turkey. 'The vegetables are stone cold,' Vida said almost with pleasure.

'You must be starved,' Ellie told him when he returned and looked at the plate.

'Not really. I—' Duke stopped in time. He must not admit he had already eaten and wonderfully enjoyed one Christmas dinner today. He said, 'I mean, yes. I am hungry. The night air gives one an appetite.'

Toby laughed. Amalie said nothing. Vida shook her head. Gormless, it was the word. But then, what came next put Duke, Amalie and their relationship out of Vida's mind. Completely. She forgot everything except herself. For it happened. A nightmare became reality and in reality it was no less an nightmare. The fear she may have had when thinking about this thing was nothing to what she felt now when it was about to come true. Well, part of it. The part about Lydia coming here.

And what timing, she might have thought if she was a woman to appreciate such things. At my own dinner table on Christmas night.

For Toby had taken an air letter from his pocket. 'This came this morning. I put it in the pocket of my grey suit and forgot about it. I remembered when I was changing. So I put it into this pocket.' Vida insisted upon black ties for this very special meal. She said it gave the occasion the right atmosphere. This was why she had frowned on Duke sitting among them in tweed jacket and polo-necked jersey. Ellie asked if the letter was from Lydia, and when Toby nodded, Ellie looked straight at Vida. And Ellie laughed.

Toby couldn't find his spectacles. Ellie went to look for them and took her time over it to torment her mother.

Christmas night, Vida thought. Peace on

81

earth and goodwill. I know what is in that letter as well as if I had read it, as if she had addressed it to me. Oh no, not to me. I just look after the place. And though I say it myself, I have never seen a place better looked after. I do everything I can for this house. But if she writes a letter, it is to Toby.

What an end to Christmas dinner! Amalie scowling across the table at that man. If she doesn't want him why doesn't she give him his marching orders? She shouldn't scowl. She isn't young and at her age the lines come fast and hard enough.

I wish Toby wouldn't sit there discussing the wine with Ben. Men are conceited about that sort of thing, precious.

Ben's dinner jacket gets shinier every time he puts it on.

Where is Ellie with those spectacles?

But at last Toby had his spectacles. Even then he went on talking about the merits of one wine against another with Ben. Then he held the bottle up. 'Vida?' 'No.' 'Amalie?' Amalie nodded. 'Ellie?' Toby asked. 'She has had enough,' Vida snapped. 'Pass your glass,' Toby told their daughter.

When their glasses were filled, he still

did not read the letter. 'Toby,' Vida said. 'What does Lydia say?'

'Oh yes.' Toby opened it and scanned it, then laid it down again beside his plate. 'As I was saying—' He turned to Ben.

'*Toby*—'

'Lydia is coming home for a bit. She will be here in a week or so. She says she is looking forward to it because she is tired of travelling.'

'Like Charles,' Duke said helpfully. They stared at him. 'The Second,' he murmured.

If Lydia, when she wrote the letter, had known the effect it would have, would she have written it? She could never have guessed what effect it would have.

5

'She is coming to take the house away from us,' Vida said.

Toby stared. 'What would she want the house for?'

'She will take it from spite,' Vida said.

And this upset Toby. He would not have sworn he was all that fond of either of the girls. But Lydia, living away from home and going her own way, gave him no trouble whereas Ellie was under his feet all day.

'Ma has been afraid of this,' Ellie said. 'She says she has seen it coming.'

'Seen what coming?' Toby asked.

'A blizzard,' Ellie elaborated. 'And Lydia turning us out in it and us having nowhere to go.'

Toby told her not to be absurd. Ellie only laughed. Vida said nothing. She had fought down her hysteria. Evidently Toby did not join her in her suspicions of Lydia so she must keep her thoughts to herself. She might want her husband to say passionately, 'No, she shall not turn you out. This is your home. You love it and serve it well.' Of course Toby would do no such thing. But if they were turned out—and it was an *idée fixe* with her now—it would be she, Vida, who would have chores to do like packing, and the awful job of moving to another place. Ben, seeing her so obviously upset, patted her hand. She wanted to hit him.

'You never know,' she heard herself say. 'Lydia may take a fancy to this place and want it for herself.'

'It is a charming house,' Duke agreed pleasantly, thinking this might be what Vida wished to hear but he was taken aback by the look of pure hatred she turned upon him.

They had brandy and liqueurs in the sitting-room. 'May I read the letter?' Vida asked. Toby said, 'Of course,' and gave it to her. But the letter gave Vida no comfort, saying as it did that Lydia was tired of travelling, the Cape was glorious but somehow had lost its appeal. 'I find I want to come home, I keep thinking about the house. I am even looking forward to snow and frost, though people here tell me I must be mad! When I come, I hope to

86

stay for a good long time.'

You should listen to those people, Vida thought.

Ellie was thrilled with the news. My sister Lydia, the Seventh Cavalry, flying to my rescue! Surely Lydia would give her the money to leave home, stake her until Ellie was settled in London. She isn't a bad sort, Lydia. It's just Ma who hates her. Ellie was quite prepared to side with Lydia in any battle that might ensue. And battle would come, no doubt about that. Vida was probably already planning strategic positions.

This Christmas night was different from other years in that there was no singing of carols around the piano when Vida played and the rest sang. Tonight she did not have the heart for it, and Toby, for one, was pleased. He always felt a fool singing the king in Wenceslas while Ellie sang the page. This had been Vida's idea for years. But tonight Christmas was going out with a whimper and Toby thanked God for it. After a time, Vida jumped up and said she could not remain idle for another minute. The dishes, she said, would not wash themselves, after which brilliant deduction she left for the kitchen. Ben went with her. 'You stay here,' Amalie ordered Duke. Ellie stayed too until Toby said, 'Aren't you going to help your mother?'

Toby sat with his eyes shut. Duke wished he could snooze but with Amalie awake it wasn't polite or politic.

So he sat staring at the fire while Amalie stared at him. She knew he had been up to something and could not wait to get out of him what it was.

Duke thought she looked attractive in the floor-length red silk skirt and the white blouse. What he did not like were the rings on each finger of each hand. He knew this was the fashion at the moment but he thought it was awful, tasteless and ostentatious. Cherry Matthews wore just one plain gold band.

His mind had been filled with thoughts of the Matthews family while he drove here. He thought of them now, again, letting the sweet amusing warm tide flow into his mind. Cherry had been thrilled when he told her he had written and had accepted a few stories. She said she had never met a writer before. When he deprecated the title, she said, 'Well, you have something published. I bet that doesn't happen to everyone.' And he thought she bet right, remembering the stories he had had rejected. But the pleasure she showed was balm after Amalie's sneers. When Cherry asked if he still wrote, and when he said no, not for a long time, she said, 'Why not? You don't mean to say you've given it up? A talent like that. I know I wouldn't stop after I had the first accepted. One would be enough. The carrot for the donkey. I should go on for ever. Besides,' she said with exquisite good sense, 'the money must be useful.'

He thought women like Cherry had the gift for making a man feel eight feet tall. Duke, in all conscience, was tall enough but after some of the things Amalie had said he might be forgiven for feeling he had shrunk. Amalie said of herself, not without pride, that she had a reputation for cutting people down to size.

And he smiled now when he recalled Will's grace before meat. 'For what we are about to receive and for the loan of the kitchen, thanks,' Will had told the Lord, and looked ceilingward to make certain the Lord knew who was speaking.

'*Duke*—' Amalie sounded shrill. This place was getting on her nerves. Toby asleep or at least neglecting his guests to the point of rudeness. Duke came to himself with a start which showed his thoughts were not on Amalie either. 'I am going upstairs,' she said. When he stood up and amiably nodded but made no move to accompany her, she said, almost hissing with impatience, 'I want to talk to you.'

Of course she got out of him what had happened. Perhaps, after all, she had cause to be angry. Many women would be angry to think that a stranger had taken over their kitchen to cook a meal in. Some women might not have minded. After all, it was Christmas. Amalie was furious. 'You really are the biggest fool—'

'Why? She didn't harm a thing. I was there, all the time.'

'You can be conned into anything.'

'You mean Cherry was casing the joint?' It didn't help, his laugh and his use of the name. 'She is no Mafia's moll, if Mafias have molls. They don't, do they? They set great store by Italian womanhood, I gather—or Sicilian—'

'Oh, shut up. And start packing.'

'I haven't unpacked. Where are we going?'

'You don't suppose I could stay here, now I know? I shouldn't have a moment's

90

peace of mind. How do you know,' Amalie said wildly, showing a side of her he didn't know existed, 'she didn't come back and ransack the place—told her pals what was in it—'

He wanted very much to say, 'Well, what is in it?' But he only said quietly, 'You are being absurd but all right, I'll come back with you.'

Vida stared in astonishment as Amalie, changed into her outdoor clothes, went in search of her to say goodbye. 'What's wrong? What has he done?' meaning Duke.

Amalie said she would tell Vida everything, later. She did not bother to say goodbye to the others but left. Duke thanked Vida for the meal and left too.

He followed Amalie in his car. He had no wish to leave the car at Vida's and fetch it some other time. They arrived in London after midnight. When she let herself into the flat, Amalie did not know what to expect. She had to admit the place looked no different but she went through every drawer and cupboard. She scoured the kitchen for signs of dirt or disorder. There was nothing. But, 'I shall have no peace until I have changed the locks,' she said. Then she took the cyclamen from its green pot and threw it on to the floor. She trod on it until it was ruined. She tore up the note Cherry had left. 'Miss Kettle. Thank you very much for the loan of the kitchen. A Happy New Year. Cherry Matthews.'

Then she stormed at Duke to get out. Amalie in a temper was an ugly woman.

He went. He did not collect any clothes, nothing like that. He drove out of town, parked in a quiet lane and sat in the car until it was light. Then, sensibly, he did what his heart told him to do. He returned to London to Cherry and the children. When she opened the door to him, she looked radiant, but said, a moment later, 'She minded?' He nodded. This was the only mention they made of it. Now it had happened, they could do nothing but spend the day together and enjoy it. They did. He saw that she was wearing the brooch.

Lydia's mother, Syb, at a New Year's party in New York, found herself confiding in the young man sitting next to her about her daughter and her daughter's problems. Syb, if asked, would say yes, she found most people *simpatico*, by which Syb might mean she pinned them down beside her and said aloud what currently went through her mind. She liked doing this for it did two things. It brought her problems out in the open and it provided conversation. Ninety-nine out of a hundred listeners were interested, flattered that this charming intelligent woman should talk to them thus, even confide in them. Sometimes, there was a bonus for her. Some one person in her audience might have something to offer. This young man did.

Syb said Lydia was going back to England. In January. 'I cannot think why. No one goes back in January, unless they have to, except perhaps for the Sales.'

He recognized a lot of what Syb said was said for effect and he smiled. He said, 'Perhaps she loves the place?'

'We all do,' Syb said. 'It doesn't mean we have to suffer for it.'

'Why isn't she here with you?'

'Because she wants to put roots down and I am a rootless person.'

He nodded.

She didn't know what this young man did for a living. When she asked about him being here, he had said he had come with a friend. And left it at that. A writer, she thought. She didn't think he was an actor. He would have talked about himself before this if he were. A writer and one who played it close to his chest and made you ask what books he had written if you didn't recognize the name. She hadn't got his name. She knew his first name was Alec but this was all. No matter. This was very much a first-name party.

He was tall and dark and good-looking, and he had good manners, she thought. He listened attentively and when he asked a question it was a sensible one. He wasn't married. She had enquired. Then she said, thinking it was time to ask, 'What do you write?'

'Reports, mostly.'

'Reports? On what?'

He said he was an accountant.

'An accountant?' Syb was thunderstruck. So much so he laughed. 'A lot of us around, these days.'

'Indeed, yes. I employ one.'

'I am sure you do.'

'Who employs you?'

He said he worked for a British firm, one of the biggest, world-wide connections. 'In trade,' he said, his eyes twinkling.

'I'm no snob,' Syb told him. 'Go where

the money is, I say. You don't look like an accountant—'

'We come in all shapes and sizes.'

'I thought you must be a writer.'

'Not a chance,' he said cheerfully. 'I have no novel I turn to when I go home, nights, half written, destined for the round of the publishers. I enjoy my work,' he said. 'If I didn't think I should, I wouldn't have taken it up.'

'What did you say your name was?'

'Alec Bartlow. I live in Hampstead.'

'They pay you well in this firm with the world-wide net?'

'A small place in Hampstead.'

'I know a man called Bartlow. Ben Bartlow. I think there is something wrong with him,' Syb said cheerfully. 'Or he suffers from appalling judgment. He is the swain of my ex-husband's present wife, Vida. Now if you saw Vida, you would know she is no Guinevere. Yet I gather Ben has been showering affection upon her for years. I cannot understand it. Not a relation of yours, I hope?' she belated said.

'Yes. A distant relative. I call him uncle but the relationship is more tortuous.'

There was silence. Then Syb said, 'I still

can't understand what he sees in her.'

'You wouldn't be biased?'

'Of course I am biased. Show me a woman who isn't biased about her ex-husband's second choice, and in my opinion she didn't care much for him to start with.' Then she said, 'When do you go back to England?'

'The second week in January.'

'Do you ever visit your uncle?'

'I don't know him.' But he knew what she wanted. When he returned to England, she wanted him to visit Uncle Ben to find out how Lydia was getting on, then report back to her. When he put this to her she nodded. He said gently, 'Why not go yourself? I am sure she would love to have you there.'

'The love would be one-sided. Not love for Lydia. But I cannot go there until the place has warmed up a bit. May, perhaps, or June.' Then she said, 'Why should someone like Vida appeal to someone like your uncle?'

'A bit of an earth-mother, is she?'

'You might call it that.'

'He must be lonely,' Alec said and told her what he knew about that side of the family. 'The upper-crust connection.

Their heyday was in Edwardian times. You know, the bit everyone drools over. After the Boer War and on to the start of the next.'

'Georgian, a bit, but I know what you mean. You don't approve?'

'It wasn't all cucumber sandwiches and the butler and footmen bringing tea beneath the cedar. It wasn't all dinners in Park Lane and the carriages waiting. There was another side. And I think it's damn silly,' he said forthrightly, 'to dwell on it while one is washing up at the sink.'

Syb only knew she herself would have revelled in the tea on the lawn and carriages in Park Lane bit. She could see herself making her way towards the cedar, two young men in attendance, her skirt trailing the grass, her hat a lyric poem. The lake, the huge trees, flower-filled urns on the terrace. And the family pile for background. 'Come away,' she heard him say. 'You are not a woman to waste time on nostalgia.'

'I shouldn't have minded being one of them. Alec, if you visit your uncle—'

'I said I don't know him.'

'Then it is time you did. When you go,

if Lydia is around—'

'Find out if she is enjoying herself?'

'More than that. Make a fuss of her.'

When he could he said, 'You mean, in the old-fashioned phrase, give her a whirl? How would she feel if she knew we were even discussing it? Planning what to do with her?' He did indeed sound incensed.

'What is best for her,' Syb corrected. 'She wouldn't resent it. She has lovely manners. She might feel a little depressed but she is honest too and would realize she has herself to blame. Here she is, twenty-five, just gone, and her mother has to ask a personable young man to call—'

Her mother has a somewhat cold heart and a turn for scheming, he thought. He said, and he sounded brusque, for the first time, 'Girls aren't like that, these days. They don't thank you for interfering.'

'When you go there,' Syb said, at her most beguiling, 'and see what it is like—'

'What do you mean? There is a Gothic element creeping in now—'

Syb said, 'Lydia thinks she is going home. That is the tenor of what she writes. She is going to be disappointed again. Toby and I have both failed her. Of course she could stay with me. I am

not a woman afraid of my own daughter.'
Indeed, Syb thought, it might be the other
way round. Poor Lydia might be snuffed
out. 'I think it best she should be on her
own. It is just that it does breed loneliness
as well as self-sufficiency. Toby doesn't
bother about her.'

She was silent, not pausing to choose
her words. To let him get the picture.
Then she continued. 'Vida is possessive.
She wants nothing to do with Lydia or
with me. She owns Toby now, so she
thinks. Perhaps she is afraid. Small-minded
people sometimes are. They seem to have
no defence. No sense of humour, either.
Lydia will learn this. She will go there
wanting to do her best in the situation,
to help, to be the daughter of the house.
She is that unhappy combination, bossy
and shy.'

'Bossy?' This was the last word he would
have thought of.

'Oh, for the best. She is not like me
who can let people stew in their own juice,'
Syb said happily. 'I have a reputation for
helping others but only if it doesn't cost me
much. But Lydia really cares if people are
happy, and she does what she can to see
that they are. Mind you, she isn't stupid.

No buying affection, no piling on of gifts to make them like her. But she is going there, I know she is, to see if anyone needs her, then by golly, she will lay about her to help. Vida won't take long to sense this. She will suspect Lydia will change the old order, sweep everything before her, that sort of thing. And Vida will fight for it not to happen.'

'You should write the books!'

'So she will need someone, Lydia, to give her a whirl, when she has been there for some time,' Syb said as if he had not spoken. 'For she will feel not wanted. Again.'

'You are trying to make me sorry for her?'

'Wrong. Try to make her see she has a duty to herself as well as to the family. You may,' Syb said, 'light something within her, some spark—'

'For God's sake—' he exclaimed.

'They would be badly written books,' Syb chuckled. 'The ones I should write. I have heard it said,' she murmured, 'my Lydia is like me without the light within her.' She looked at him with a certain triumph. 'Maybe a visit from a personable young man would change her—'

'You want her lit up?'

'I shouldn't mind.'

'I haven't said I shall go there.'

'Of course you will,' she said happily. 'Now you know all this. "That girl", you will say to yourself. "I wonder what she is really like?"'

'I may have a girl of my own.'

'I am sure you have.'

'Not at the moment,' he had to admit: 'By mutual consent.'

'Good. Now I am not asking you to make Lydia fall in love with you.'

He told her he was delighted to hear it.

'But try to go there. Tell her you are a friend of mine. After you have paid respects to Ben, of course. Make a fuss of her. Let Vida see you do it.'

'I'll get you a drink,' he said. 'After all this talk, you must be thirsty.'

But before he could rise, she put a hand on his arm and kept him beside her for a few more moments. 'Not a monster,' she said. 'A mother. I don't want Vida taking it out on my ewe lamb.'

6

Lydia arrived early in January. January can be a miserable month, not necessarily waist-deep in drifts but monotonously grey and dank. Victorian laurel time, Syb Farmer called it. Weather that complemented the yellow and green shrubs beloved of our forebears. Syb hated them.

Lydia drove to Wadden in the car she had hired until she decided what to buy. Vida opened the door to her. They stood looking at one another. Vida greeted her, then said, 'Your father is in London for a couple of days. If you had only let us know when you were coming he might have put the dentist off. But perhaps not. I should have liked to know, though. A telephone call,' she said, 'wouldn't have cost much time or money.'

Heart, ordered Lydia, don't sink.

'I'm sorry. I think I wanted to surprise you. You got my letter?'

'It upset my Christmas.'

'*Why?*'

Vida only said she didn't like surprises, letters arriving out of the blue to say people were coming. But, thinking she had managed to get this girl off on the wrong foot, so to speak, she cheered up. 'Is that your car?' When Lydia explained, 'How long do you plan to stay?' Vida asked but didn't wait for an answer. She said, 'Well, come in. Is that all the luggage you have? One suitcase and a holdall?' When Lydia said the rest were coming by sea, Vida said, 'What have you got, then?'

'Bits and pieces I have collected.' Lydia's tone was cooler. You did not have to be greatly sensitive to recognize this wasn't much of a welcome, there would be no fatted calf.

But, once inside, she had to say how greatly she admired the hall. She did. It was charming. Green growing plants, a pretty Chinese screen. Two carved lacquer chests, red and gold. A huge vase with writhing dragons. 'Drat—' Vida said, rushing over to the vase. 'Toby will use it as an umbrella stand.' She hauled out the offending umbrella.

Lydia thought she looked amusing, standing there, short, dumpy, clutching the large black umbrella. But it wouldn't do to smile. She repeated how pretty the hall was. Vida said nothing. Lydia asked after Ellie. 'Ellie is at work. Some people have to work. You don't mine coming into the kitchen? It's my baking day.'

'Do you entertain much?' Lydia asked as she followed Vida down the passage. 'No,' Vida said. 'It's too much trouble.'

And that was that.

It seemed hard for Lydia not to say the wrong thing, not to drop a clanger, a word which had suddenly come into her mind from schooldays. When she said what a pretty warm kitchen it was and what a long time since she herself had been in a kitchen, Vida said some people didn't know how lucky they were.

You don't have to have a step-mother out of Grimm. Lydia thought.

But the tea was hot and the fresh cinnamon buns delicious. Lydia ate two. 'You'll put on weight,' Vida said.

'I seem to be one of the lucky ones. I eat what I like and stay slim.'

'It won't last. Don't bank on staying thin. I was like you once but not now. I think,' Vida said, 'I shall be like the Queen Mother. Pretty but plump.'

There wasn't much Lydia could say to this. Vida, her last cake safely in the oven, said directly, 'What made you come back?'

'I told Toby. I was tired of travelling, bored with it.'

'At your age, you should be interested in everything,' Vida said. 'You shouldn't admit to feeling bored. If you stay here, you will be bored. Even Ellie complains and she has lots of friends. Don't say I didn't warn you. I give you a couple of weeks before you will be heading back to London and what I believe are called the bright lights.'

'I don't think they call them that any more,' Lydia said coolly. 'And I think you are wrong.' Then she stopped, staring at the man who stood in the doorway. The overall effect was a handsome old man, blue-eyed, erect, a bit of a dandy. But a man who was looking at her in such obvious dislike she wondered what was wrong with him, for to her knowledge they had never met. He scowled as if the sight of her offended him. Ben knew her from photographs. She had no idea who he was.

He refused tea and marched out. Vida laughed.

'What have I ever done to him or does he just object to visitors?' Like you, Lydia wanted to add.

'Oh—' Vida waved a hand, gave no explanation. 'Ben lives with us. Ben Bartlow. I hope,' she piously said, 'he lives here until he passes on.'

She paused as people do to give the phrase full weight. 'He has no one else.'

'No family?'

'What use is family?' Vida said. She really was a strange woman. She made it plain she did not want in the family this girl sitting here with her; at the same time there was in her tone a wealth of condemnation against those who would not take to their bosom old men like Ben.

Dear Ben, he can't hide his feelings. He knows how upset the thought of this girl makes me. He knows what I am afraid of and how unfair it is I should be badgered thus.

More to the point, Vida briskly thought, he knows that if we go, he may have nowhere to live. If we have to move to a smaller place, I expect he is asking himself if there will be room there for him.

'I have put you in the best guest room,' she said.

The guest room. That is what I am offered in what I thought is my home. But it isn't home, Lydia told herself. I know that now, in the first half hour. It is nothing I dreamed it would be. So much for dreams. It is a house where my father lives, a house I own when I remember I do.

'What are you thinking about?' Vida said. Lydia answered truthfully, 'I was thinking how strange it is that I own this house. I never think about it.'

She could have said nothing calculated to worry Vida more. There was silence until Vida said, 'I'll show you your room.'

'You must let me help with the work.'

'It's quicker to do it myself.' Then Vida said, as Lydia followed her out of the kitchen, into the hall and up the stairs, 'You are like your mother to look at.'

It was true. Opening the front door to this girl had been like opening it to Syb. Tall, slim, dark. Well-dressed. Expensive-looking was how Vida described it. Syb had always been expensive-looking. But perhaps, Vida thought, Syb's daughter would be easier to handle. If Syb were here, battle would be joined by now. Or Vida would have had to make the effort

108

to sound welcoming. She said, 'Does your mother know you are here?'

'Yes.'

'Doesn't she want you with her?'

'I'm a big girl now.'

'Ellie would always want to be with me.'

'Well, good for Ellie.'

The best guest room was the only guest room of any size, the other being more of a box room. This was the room Amalie and Duke had when they were here. Lydia stood by the window. Naturally, at this time on a January afternoon, she could see nothing. But in the spring and summer it must be charming. When she said so, Vida said, with a certainty that was aggravating, 'Oh, you won't be here then. You will get fed up with it long before.'

Lydia turned from the window, took a deep breath, and asked after Vida's sister.

'Amalie. Her name is Amalie. Distinctive, isn't it? Not like Emily. When there were parlour-maids, they were usually Emily. Or Sarah. Amalie?' Vida repeated, coming back to the present. 'Oh, she is doing splendidly. But then, she is a clever woman. And not one of your drones, you know. She is secretary to a tycoon.' And she went on to describe, fully and at length, Amalie's capabilities.

When she paused for breath, Lydia said, 'And not married, yet?'

Vida glanced sharply at her. A glimpse, after all, of Syb? You never knew with these quiet ones. No, she said, Amalie was still single. 'There is a man who wants to marry her but to tell you the truth I hope Amalie gives him his marching orders. I wish, every time she telephones, that is what she will say. But she is too soft hearted. He isn't worthy of her, not a patch on her. When they marry it is she who will keep him. What kind of life is that? Do you know what job he had at Christmas?'

'Santa Claus in a department store,' Lydia said. She went on to say it was a job she herself would love. 'All those confidences—'

'You are talking nonsense. It's not the sort of job where you get your picture in the business page of the Dailies. Amalie's boss has his picture there, quite often. Keen looking. Well, I shall leave you to unpack.'

'Do you,' Lydia forced herself to ask, 'change for dinner?'

But Vida took it seriously. 'Not a black tie, no. But I myself have never sat down to the meal in the clothes I wore in the kitchen, if you understand. None of your gaudy efforts. But yes, something—'

'Dainty?' Lydia devilishly asked. She could not remember having used the word in her life before. Vida nodded.

Maybe, Lydia thought when she was on her own, things will cheer up a bit when Toby is back. It had been a bitter disappointment to find him absent.

For the evening meal, Lydia took thought and changed into a long black skirt of fine wool with bobbles round the hem and a white silk shirt. Silver hoops in her ears and her hair in two wings on her cheeks. She thought she was ready for anything from dinner-table chat to washing up.

When she went downstairs and back into the kitchen, Ellie was there. Ellie had been late arriving home from work, her mother was not to know she had been having a couple of drinks in the pub, and had not yet greeted her half-sister. She did now by taking one look and putting her hand over her eyes, in an exaggerated pose as if blinded by a vision. 'My God—'

'Stop that blasphemy,' Vida ordered.

111

'Good Lord,' Ellie said obediently and insolently. 'Lydia thinks she is back in South Africa. She has come to the kitchen door to tell the cook what time she wants the meal. *Dinner at half-past-seven, missus?'* Ellie said in ridiculous mimicry.

Then she came at Lydia with a rush, put her arms round her and kissed her, whispered fiercely, 'I could kill you for looking like this.'

'You have all the aces,' Lydia said.

'What are they?'

'*Youth.* In seven years you will be my age, and I shall be thirty-two.'

'It's no comfort now, all that arithmetic.' Ellie had to finger the silver hoops, feel the expensive skirt between thumb and finger. 'Useful for travelling,' Lydia said, feeling she had to say something. 'It packs small and doesn't crease.'

'I wouldn't know. I don't go anywhere,' Ellie told her.

Here it is, she thought, walking into my life like something out of *Vogue*. My great chance. My escape route. Lydia, my half-sister. Lydia has plenty of money. She looks easy-going, positively soft. I should be able to touch her for the money to get away. She looks a bit out of place too. I don't suppose Ma rolled out the red carpet, not even the mat with Welcome on it.

I should like to take you in hand, Lydia thought. I should take you to a good hairdresser to style that hair. It doesn't suit you long like that. If you don't want it cut I should buy you a packet of hair pins. You could pin it up. You look like a panda with that dated eye make-up. I should tell you to stand up straight. But if I sound unkind I would buy you your own evening skirt and blouse and silver earrings. And burn the flared pants and the tank top over the wrong sort of shirt.

They smiled at one another.

Dinner passed off fairly well. Lydia thought Ben had come to grips with the situation now. At least he did not look as if he were contemplating grinding glass on her behalf. He wore a frilled shirt and a velvet jacket.

'Amalie will wish to meet you as soon as possible,' Vida said. 'I'll ask her up, the weekend after next. I suppose he will have to come.'

'I thought, at Christmas, he had managed to give her the slip,' Ellie said. 'Amalie's kept man,' she told Lydia.

This earned a rebuke from Vida that Lydia thought was richly deserved. She thought Ellie's pertness singularly unattractive. Anyway, it sat uneasily with the long hair and sulky mouth.

'I have never known Amalie when she wasn't criticizing something or someone,' Ellie went on, undeterred. 'Me, usually. I don't take much notice now but when I was a kid it was purgatory. Particularly when I was at school. She wanted to know who my friends were to make certain I wasn't wasting my time on anyone I couldn't name drop.'

'I don't understand half you say,' Vida told her. 'But if your aunt did criticize, it was for your good.'

God forbid, Ellie thought. Then she thought she couldn't see Amalie having children. And God be thanked. Those nippers are better off unborn. Catching Vida's eye, she gave her mother a pretty little wink. Indulgently, Vida laughed. 'We are really a happy little family,' Vida said. Then she told Lydia the story of Duke and the goose which episode Amalie had passed on to her as she had promised. Lydia thought it delightful but prudently said nothing. She was learning.

'It cooked his goose,' Ellie said as she was bound to say. 'Amalie turned him out. But she took him back. She has no one else.'

'Ellie—' This was her mother. Vida said, 'But as long as Amalie's good nature gets the better of her, she will meet no one else. It is very selfish of that man to stay there.'

Ellie smiled at Lydia who smiled back.

I wonder if she has any clothes she is tired of, Ellie asked herself, worn once and discarded. She sighed for the fortunate state of some people.

Of course Duke had gone back to Amalie and the flat. Cherry knew that he would. And Cherry knew something else, that never, since Bert died, had she met a man who made her feel like this tall red-haired man she had not known existed before Christmas, and whom she now knew she would never forget. For he had the effect of lifting from Cherry's heart the burden of fear that lay there. No one, seeing Bert Matthew's widow, would have guessed she was afraid. She hid it well. This is what they said about her. 'Brave little thing. She took it well.'

Perhaps. She herself sometimes thought she had not 'taken it' all that well if she still lived under this cloud of fear. Nothing specific, there was nothing, no situation even, she could point at and say, 'I fear that happening.' It was rather a feeling of heaviness, apprehension, of something lurking around the corner with which she might not be able to cope and which would make her pretence that she had everything under control, that she was coping well, collapse like the flimsy thing she sometimes thought it was.

Of course, having the children was the most wonderful thing, the best thing for her. You did not have all that much time to worry in. But the children went to bed early and the evenings were long, the nights lonely. Lucy was a darling, Will a corker. Will was the man about the house but Cherry did not want him to become a little old man, old before his time through shouldering burdens.

And then, at Christmas, Duke came into her life. Like an Angel with a Flaming Sword, she extravagantly thought, putting an end to fear, killing it dead by his thoughtfulness and friendliness, by his presence there in the kitchen where he drank his tea and talked and laughed and made her laugh as if they had known one another all their lives. Was she in love with him? All she knew was that when she was with him she was a different person, happy and gay again.

But of course, she told herself, even if she were in love with him, she didn't stand a chance for there was a young lady he belonged to. (Cherry was given sometimes to curiously old-fashioned phrases. But when she had seen a photograph of Amalie, there in the flat, she had thought this indeed was a young lady, in the phrase she meant, who would not give up what was hers without a fight. Coming back to today, *hard as nails*, Cherry thought.)

So Duke went back to the flat and when Amalie saw him she laughed and said, 'You fool—' and, for her, that was that. But Duke meant to go on seeing Cherry Matthews and the children because he was certain Cherry needed company. He liked her too. He hoped she knew this.

He thought it could be managed. What the outcome would be he didn't ask himself, not at this stage. After Christmas he found a job in a book store opposite the shop where he had played at Santa Claus and when he looked across the street at the great plate glass windows and let his eye travel upwards to the third floor, he saw it all again. The gold and scarlet throne and himself in red with a fur trim, the white beard. He heard the blue-birds twitter and saw the goldfish in the pool, parrots and monkeys and reindeer. 'Pack it all in,' the designer had said. 'Kids love it all. You can't give 'em too much, not real kids.' Lucy and Will were real kids, the hard-eyed formidable boy and the enchanting little girl. 'Do you still want that stove?' he had asked Cherry after Christmas. She had shaken her head, smiling, but not saying what was in her heart. 'Don't stop coming, though.' He hadn't said he would still come. He thought she would understand that he would.

And he started writing again. He wrote the story of Absalom, the Christmas Goose. At least, he wrote the first draft. He would rewrite it many times before eventually sending it off to a magazine which accepted it for their Christmas issue. He didn't tell Amalie but read it aloud to Cherry who laughed until tears came. 'Don't you dare *not* send that off,' she said.

When Toby Farmer returned to the house from London he looked surprised to find Lydia there. 'You knew I was coming,' she told him. 'But it is as I told you, Lydia,' Vida said before Toby could say a word. 'You didn't give us a date. You just turned up. Out of the blue. You should have given us a date.' When Vida got hold of a word she hammered it to death.

When they were alone, Lydia and Toby, he did ask what she would find to do here. Can't I just be part of the family? she wanted to know. He said he supposed so, though he sounded dubious. It wasn't, he implied, as if she and Ellie could go to the beach and bathe and make sand pies together. Not at their age. 'Nothing much here for you. Do you play golf?'

'Badly.' Then she said, not without irony, 'I shall try to be no trouble. I just wanted to come home.'

'Most girls want to travel,' Toby said. 'Rum world, ain't it?'

That night, in bed, Vida said, 'Toby?'
'What?'
'Already, Lydia has offered to get the sitting-room redecorated. I just happened

119

to mention the paper needed changing, that I was tired of the pattern, and she upped and said, "Get it done." In the spring, she has plans for the garden. She wants to give me a dishwasher.'

'Then grab it. You've been on about one for years.' Toby was tired. He didn't want pillow chat.

'Toby, do you think it's the thin edge of the wedge? The foot in the door?'

'What door?'

'The sitting-room door, if you like. Lydia is getting the house done up as she likes it. Then she will take it over.'

'Are you still on that lark?' he demanded. 'When you meet Lydia tomorrow, at breakfast, ask her if she has come here to turn us out. Say that is what you suspect—'

'I can't. I should feel embarrassed.'

'I should think so. Go to sleep,' he told her. 'If she wants the house, she will find somewhere else for us to live. She's like that. Generous. But maybe you are right. Maybe there is a man somewhere she wants to marry and she does plan to live here. Like mother, like daughter. Syb had the house ready for her and me. Very useful it was.'

'I don't want another house. I love this house. I don't want to be turned out. Toby,' she said, 'don't go to sleep. I want to talk to you.'

Not that night.

Amalie, hearing that Lydia had arrived, was agog to meet her. But Lydia was with Toby in Wadden looking for a car to suit her needs when the visitors arrived from London. When Lydia returned, Amalie was with Vida in the kitchen, hearing Vida's account of what had happened in the past ten days.

When Lydia went up to her room she threw coat and bag on to the bed. There was a muttered sound. She switched on the light.

On the bed a red-haired man lay stretched out, asleep. At least he had been sleeping until the bag bounced on his chest.

7

And this was how Lydia Farmer met Duke. He opened his eyes, stared at her, blinked, murmured, 'Good heavens, the wrong girl—' and jumped off the bed. He looked so much like a temporarily bewildered giraffe that she smiled deeper than was her wont in this house. 'I am sorry,' Duke said. She thought he had a lovely voice. 'We always have this room. But of course you are Miss Farmer—'

'Lydia, yes.'

'Thank you. Duke Beverley. I don't think Hollywood could think up anything jazzier.'

'Children must like using it,' Lydia said. 'They love anything tuppence coloured.'

'By jove,' he told her, 'you're right. I never thought of it. But kids do say, "Is that your real name?" and when I say it is, they say, "It's smashing".' He smiled at her. A Duke special. He was at the door now and said, 'I shall see you at dinner.'

'But dinner is hours off. Don't you take

tea?' Lydia didn't always take tea here but with Duke for company she thought she might.

But they had no chance of getting to know one another at tea for Amalie was there and hogged both conversation and guest. If Vida was like a puff ball, Lydia thought Amalie a string bean. Too thin. Too glossy, altogether, a gloss that came from a careful search for what was smart, today, someone else's originality snatched and worn like hand-me-downs. The eyes assessed.

Amalie accurately priced Lydia's skirt, cashmere jersey and suède boots, all in a shade of cream. But Amalie was determined not to be impressed. Not at first. She was when Lydia mentioned where and when she had met Amalie's boss and his wife. 'J.G., you mean?'

Lydia laughed. 'Is that what you call him? His wife calls him Geraint. Lovely Welsh name.'

'Well, the staff can't call him Geraint,' Amalie snapped. 'Where did you meet him? South Africa?'

Lydia said yes. 'Early last year. They do that, don't they? The business man's special. A flight from the rigours of a

124

northern winter to South Africa or the Antipodes.'

'I really think one should not criticize,' Amalie said. 'Ordinary people have not the slightest idea of the strain our top executives live under.'

Lydia waited for the latest coronary statistics but they didn't come. She did say mildly why criticize? It was a clever thing, two birds with one air ticket. A holiday in the sun and a working session.

'Where did you meet him?' Amalie asked.

'I was staying with friends outside Johannesburg. They spent a weekend there,' Lydia told her, and, though Amalie angled busily, she never did tell her who the friends were. Perhaps she had her loyalities too. She said gently, but with malice, for she was certain Amalie's J.G. hid his wife from such as Amalie, 'His wife is delightful, isn't she?'

'A charming woman,' said Amalie, who had never met her.

'Enid—' Lydia murmured. 'So fortuitous —with Geraint.'

Amalie did not know what on earth she was talking about.

'After staying in the Transvaal, she took

a house at the coast,' Lydia said in her soft pretty voice. 'At Hermanus. The children came out for the Easter holidays. You should try to go there,' she told Duke. 'The fishing is marvellous. Then Geraint went on to Australia—'

'Of course.' Amalie's voice had the crack of an impatient bullet.

'That is not how life is meant to be lived.' Now Vida put in her penn'orth. 'Catching planes. Renting houses. You need a home of your own, Lydia. You need a base.' Ellie, who was sitting next to her mother on the sofa, bent towards Vida, pretended to nuzzle her mother's neck, but murmured wickedly. 'Anywhere but here.'

There were times when Vida wished Ellie was young enough to be smacked again.

But now Amalie had decided that Lydia was a darling person, one of the nicest. Someone indeed to be cultivated. Did she not know J.G. and Enid? 'Will you visit from here?' she asked. Adding, as she must, 'They live in Wiltshire.'

'But Enid is in Canada,' Lydia said, smiling. 'Had you forgotten? She has gone to visit her mother there. My mother met her in New York. Syb liked her very much.' But scoring off a snob like Amalie did nothing to make Lydia feel eight feet tall. It was like taking candy from a baby. Amalie, all weekend, pestered Lydia to come to London and stay with her. 'A few days. I can get tickets for any show you want to see. Some shopping? By this time, surely you want to shop?' Amalie never gave up. 'I'll telephone,' Lydia said, weakly. 'In a week or two.' Syb would have said, 'I can't be certain of bringing Enid.' But then, Lydia wasn't Syb.

So Amalie and Duke left and Lydia was sorry to see him go. She had not had much chance to talk or get to know him but somehow his presence was comforting. When the word entered her mind, she asked herself why she needed comfort in so short a time? Perhaps she needed to feel she was liked by someone. It was as stark as that. She knew Vida did not like her and did not want her here. Ellie was friendly. But there was a greater difference than the age gap between her and Ellie. Ellie seemed to belong to a world Lydia knew nothing about when she was at home. Mother love must make Vida blind, Lydia thought, not to see that

Ellie is a devious girl, downright false. Still, that had nothing to do with her. She wasn't likely to be asked to side with Ellie or Vida. Ben, by this time, had overcome his first unfriendliness. But Ben went his own way.

Toby had been the greatest disappointment.

Well, what did you expect, she asked herself. I didn't expect, in all truth, he would be quite so indifferent to my being here. Toby gave no indication that he was pleased or not with the visit his older daughter was paying him, the distance she had come, the trouble taken. Toby was pleasant but did not go out of his way with Lydia.

He had always been more than willing to leave the girls to their mothers. After all, this was a woman's job. He supposed that if Lydia or Ellie got into any kind of trouble he might do something, if he had to. But then, any trouble they might find themselves in would be the sort Syb or Vida could cope with. When he thought about it, it did occur to him he had married capable women, both times.

'When are you getting married?' he

128

asked Lydia. 'Girls marry young, these days, so I hear.'

'You mean I am getting long in the tooth for it?'

'You are. But what's stopping you? You have the money,' he said frankly. 'Like your mother before you.'

'I have to find the right man.'

'That's true,' Toby agreed. 'But don't leave it too late.'

'You mean you would like to be a grandfather?'

He said he hadn't given it a thought and she believed him.

When Syb telephoned from New York, she wanted to know all Lydia had done and seen since she arrived. Lydia could not dissemble so Syb said, 'It doesn't sound as if you've done much.'

'I like it here.'

'Yes,' her mother said. 'There are some pleasant walks in the neighbourhood. Lydia, it's time you left.'

'I've only just come.'

'You've seen what it is like.'

But Lydia said she would stay on and Syb, after losing her temper and getting nowhere, regained composure and said that of course Lydia was to take her time but not to take too long to be a target for Vida's slings and arrows.

'That was *outrageous fortune*—'

'Maybe that's what you are getting there.'

But Lydia was stubborn. She had come all this way winged, as it were on hope. She would leave when she was ready.

She called on the Ellworthys who rented the house at the top of the hill, a house very different from the sturdy stone house near the road. This second house wore almost a Mediterranean air, painted white with green shutters, having a glassed-in veranda from which there was an exhilarating view of the estuary and the sea. Lydia thought it must be lovely in summer. She enjoyed her visit. Mrs Ellworthy told her she was the best sort of landlord, one who never interfered. As tenants, Lydia thought, they were first class. The house was well looked after. It had a loved look. When she said this, Mrs Ellworthy agreed they had enjoyed their stay here but had to say they were leaving for Bermuda where their daughter lived. 'You might come here yourself,' she suggested. 'I cannot imagine you sharing the house below, all summer. You would like it here. When you look down from the verandah you can imagine yourself monarchs of all you survey. *From the centre all round to the sea I am lord of the fowl and the brute.'* Her lanquid drawl made a pretty nonsense of the words, and Lydia laughed.

Laugh if you like, thought her companion, but living with that woman there below I should think you need a bolt hole. Vida and Mrs Ellworthy cordially disliked one another. 'These retired Army types—' Vida said. 'The little woman at the bottom,' was how Mrs Ellworthy described her.

'It's a good idea,' Lydia agreed when she had thought it over. 'I came here telling myself I was coming home—' She paused. No need to go into what she had found when she came.

'More fun to make a home for yourself,' said the kind older woman.

But she suggested Lydia did not tell Vida yet that they were leaving, and she gave no reason for this. Lydia understood. Vida probably had some friend Vida herself would love to offer the house to.

I could do something with that girl if I had time, Mrs Ellworthy thought, watching

Lydia walk down the hill. *Men are so slow.* Marriage, she meant.

The next week, though early February, was a day snatched from spring. The sun was warm, the sky blue, the sea was a harebell colour. It was a day Lydia had dreamed of and waited for. When she said something of this to Vida, at breakfast, Vida said, 'You shouldn't have come if you feel the cold.'

It was early to weed the flower bed beneath the windows at the side of the house but it was a day when people do this, revelling in the softness and pale light of the sun, knowing perhaps the next time they garden will be March but nonetheless making a start which is what they call it. Lydia was lost to the world when a voice said at her back, 'Miss Farmer?' She didn't hear him. He repeated her name. She turned, apologized, stood to face him. 'I'm sorry. I was lost to the world.'

'Gardening is like that,' he said. 'What do people think of when they garden? What were you thinking of?'

'Is this a survey?'

'No. I'm curious. Because I've seen that lost-to-the-world look before now. I wondered why.'

'The mind's eye,' she said, 'seeing things as they will be in May or June. Otherwise it could not be borne. The weed-pulling.'

Over jeans she wore a blue shirt and pullover. Her hair lay on one shoulder in a plait. Alec thought she looked like the Head's favourite pupil, head girl, no doubt. But he recognised what her mother had meant. Seeing Lydia you were reminded of Syb but there was a lot different from Syb, the dancing delight Syb seemed to show in what went on, whether she really was interested or not. This girl was probably more honest than her mother and did not hide so well what she felt. If Syb were here, the ice would be truly cracked by now. With Lydia, there was a coolness, no thawing yet. She was polite but not over friendly. The smile was guarded and this gave her a stand-offish look, he thought, which might not be meant.

Her mother had said she was shy and perhaps her mother was right. Even in today's brash and brazen world there are pockets of resistance.

When he introduced himself she said Ben was in the village with Vida. They would be back soon. She invited him into the house. She took him straight to the kitchen, as Vida had taken her, put the kettle on and made tea. They sat companionably at the table and he was glad to see the shyness ease. He thought she was a girl who had been on her own for too long. What was the phrase? Knocking around the world. Lydia could afford to do it in the most comfortable way but on your own it is still a lonely thing.

'An accountant.' She smiled when she said it, and he told her that was one of the gentler reactions he had received. 'Which range from, "I don't believe it. You look human." to "How awful for you—"'

'If I were a man, I think I should like it. The simplicity and the discipline of figures.'

'If you think that way, why not—?'

'Oh no,' she said, and that was that, and he did not pursue it. Obviously she was no career girl. He wasn't sorry. There were enough of them around for one, Lydia Farmer, to opt out. He wondered how much her attitude engendered criticism. A good bit, he would think. People would say she was lazy, idle. Others would say that she was lucky, no need to earn a living. He expected she had been told to her face many a time what other

134

people thought. They are quick to do it. So he himself said nothing about careers or life work but told her why he was here. He had a week off and meant to spend it in the country, walking when the weather was good, enjoying hotel life when it rained.

'Enjoying it?' She made a face.

'Very much,' he said firmly. 'The food is good, and they have the largest collection of paperback detective novels I have ever seen. I have found some I didn't know existed.' They discovered they had mutual admiration for the *genre*. While swopping names and titles, friendship was born.

Then Vida and Ben returned. Small wonder Ben had no idea who the visitor was. But he seemed pleased. Vida pretended to be thrown into a tizz both by the arrival of the visitor and by the fact that Lydia was entertaining him in the kitchen. 'But you gave me tea here,' Lydia said. Vida snapped that this was different. 'You are family.' Alec thought she looked and sounded, at the moment, like one of the more unattractive types of terrier. 'And you in those clothes,' she told Lydia. 'You look like a tramp.'

Syb should hear you, Alec thought.

135

'Go and change,' Vida ordered. 'I'll put tea in the living-room. If I am not here to see to everything—'

Bossy little tyrant, Alec thought she was. He wondered why Lydia stayed. And what in hell did his uncle see in Vida? She was no Iseult to his Tristram. A cushy billet, was it? Well, you couldn't blame a man Ben's age for hanging on to a degree of comfort.

'Where are you staying?' Vida asked. 'At The George? I know Major Morris. I'll ring him up and tell him to take special care of you.'

'You do that,' Alec drawled in a voice suddenly very like his uncle's.

Then Vida asked what he did for a living. When he told her, 'An accountant? What a peculiar thing to be,' she said. She saw Lydia bite her lip and Vida said, 'Why are you laughing? What have I said that is funny?'

'Only that Alec was telling me earlier of people's reaction to the word—' Lydia said.

'And yours is typical,' Alec told her sunnily.

'Well, an accountant,' Vida persisted. 'Snooping into people's Tax Returns. Is that what you do? A touch of the Gestapo, it seems to me.'

But Alec had turned to Ben and deliberately began to talk about the family. It was rude, he knew it was, and he didn't give a damn.

When the visit was at an end, he said to his uncle, 'See me to the gate.' He thanked Vida for her hospitality. Then asked Lydia if she would have dinner with him, the next night. 'I'll fetch you.'

'There's a little place the other side of Wadden,' Vida said. 'I hear it's excellent.' Alec waited until she had finished, then said, 'I think I'll take you up on your offer to phone Major Morris at The George. Tell him to put on something special in Lydia's honour.'

When they reached the car, Ben said, 'Nice vehicle—' and walked round it, admiring. So Alec could do nothing but invite his uncle for a run to the coast. Ben got in with alacrity. He settled himself comfortably beside the driver and prepared to enjoy himself.

But first Alec had to say what stuck in his mind like a burr. 'Lydia Farmer—has she upset you? You don't seem to approve. I can't see anything to disapprove of.'

137

'It's Vida,' Ben said. And went on to explain about Vida being afraid the house might be snatched from her. 'Can't hide my feelings towards the gel. Has enough, heaven knows. She could buy a place of her own. But Vida is really on tenterhooks. Not the same place since that gel came—'

'For God's sake,' Alec said, outraged. 'You can't believe that. Anyone less like a turner-outer it would be hard to find. That girl would go out into the snow herself before she sent you lot.'

Ben didn't answer. When he spoke it was to say that if he could afford a car he would buy one like this.

Alec, calming down, perhaps surprised at his instant partisanship of this girl he had so recently met, asked Ben if he had ever met Syb. No, Ben had not met her. 'But you've heard of her from Vida,' Alec supplied before his uncle could say it. 'I met her in New York.'

Then Ben did come into his own. He didn't talk about Vida or Syb or anyone but himself and the people he had met and known in New York when he visited there in the Twenties and Thirties. In a flow the words came out and Alec enjoyed listening.

Here was no bore nailing you down and reminiscing. Ben was witty, amusing, even outrageous. It was like every autobiography of that period come to life. He gave flesh and blood to names Alec had only heard of. And Alec was impressed. When Ben had finished, he opened his mouth to say something but Ben forestalled him. 'Don't say it. Don't say I should write a book. Too many damn' scribblers about now. Let a politician lose his seat and what does he do? Write a book. Before long,' Ben sneered, 'you will have to write a book to say why you wrote a book. Not me. Dear boy,' he said, 'I like *to see* the effect of what I say. I like to hear people laugh at my jokes. You can't be certain they do with a book.'

'Do you ever tell Vida any of this?'

'No. She hasn't time to listen. I tell you what I do,' he said. 'I send myself to sleep thinking back on the old days. I shut my eyes and there they are, the people I knew, and there I am, both watching them and among them. Better than a night-cap. Though Toby usually invites me for a night-cap. Good sort, Toby. I have a fantastic memory,' Ben said with no false modesty. 'I remember my own life, and I remember what my mother told me about her life. Even you,' he said with a glance at his companion, 'will know a little about what my mother's life was like.'

'Indeed, yes. But I still wish all that wouldn't go to the grave with you.'

'There are some would say it was the best place for it.' Then, 'Are you happy, dear boy?'

'Yes.' Then, as most of us do today, in this world only too wickedly ready to tilt the see-saw and down we go, he amended it to, 'I think so.'

'We never said that,' Ben told him. 'Never qualified it. Maybe we weren't any happier but we believed we were. Why aren't you married?'

'Looking for the right girl.'

'You'll compromise,' Ben said.

'What do people wear to dine at The George?' Lydia asked Ellie.

'All you've got. Have you brought the family jewels?'

'Some of them,' Lydia said, patting the ball back into Ellie's court. They were sitting in Lydia's room. Lydia did not particularly wish Ellie there while she got ready for the evening, but Ellie showed no signs of leaving so Lydia put up with it.

'Wear them, then.'

'Here in the wilds?'

'You know,' Ellie chuckled, 'that is the first derogatory thing I've heard you say since you came.'

'It slipped out. I quite like the place.'

'Well, don't let Ma hear you call it that. This is the hub of the universe for Mrs Toby Farmer. Little fish,' Ellie said. She watched while Lydia changed into a short black chiffon dress, the skirt tiers of pleated frills, the bodice held by shoe string straps. She wore a diamond spray in her hair and matching earrings. 'Are those really yours?' Ellie asked. 'Or borrowed from your mother?'

'She gave them to me.'

'Cor—' Ellie said. Lydia laughed. Then Ellie said, 'I want to talk to you. About something important to me.'

'Of course. Any time.'

'Lydia, why aren't you married?'

'I haven't met the right man.'

'Well, all this money—' Ellie said. 'Some men would find it attractive.'

'I don't have to buy a man,' Lydia said mildly.

She enjoyed the evening with Alec Bartlow. The food was excellent, the service good. Neither one knew nor cared if Vida had talked to Major Morris.

Alec talked about Syb which he knew was what Lydia wanted to hear. When he said, 'Why don't you join her?' he believed he did not have to end the sentence for her to understand fully. 'Why don't you join her—it would be more fun than staying here?'

She tried to make him understand. 'Like most people, I have to live my own life. I am trying to find out what it is. At first I wanted to travel and I did travel and it was wonderful. It hasn't palled, exactly, seeing those places one has read about and wanted to see, seeing them for the first time. But it isn't a way of life. Is it? One would feel like a snail with its house on its back if one did nothing else but travel. So I came back home. I thought I might like it here.'

'Do you?'

'I don't think I am wanted at home,' she said. 'But I hope my life can be lived in England because I was right to think it

142

was the place I really loved. I do. I want to stay.'

'I'm glad.'

She smiled and thanked him. He thought she was most attractive of all when she smiled. She was an elegant young woman, beautifully dressed, with charm and grace. But she did not smile over often and when she did it was a warm, sincere smile. She said, 'There must be many people who envy me. I know they do and I understand. It looks a marvellous life, enough money to do what you wish. Then there are those who say I am lazy, that I should use what talents I have. But I know I couldn't write or paint or act. I don't want to work in an office—'

'I can't see you there.'

'Well, there you are,' she said. 'Pipped before I start. There are so many clever girls around today—'

He nodded and sighed. He knew a good many of them. Clever girls and girls clever enough to give the impression they were clever. To be truthful, he had had his fill.

He heard her say she didn't want to play at a job, fill in time. 'I know what I want to do and I shan't play at that. I shall give it everything I've got to make a success of it.'

'What is it?'

'I want to marry,' she said honestly and with such sweetness he warmed towards her. 'I can think of nothing better than bringing up a family happily, and—and for the best. Does that sound hopelessly old-fashioned?'

More like a drink of water to a thirsty man, he thought. He shook his head.

'That is why,' Lydia said, 'I have to find out what sort of person I myself am. I can't find it out by dashing from port to port or airfield to airfield. I have to take time off and live quietly and work things out. Otherwise,' she said with exquisite honesty and a quaint turn of phrase, 'he might be getting a pig in a poke. The man who marries me.'

His shout of laughter made heads turn.

Alec, by the end of the meal, found himself asking her to get in touch with him when she came up to town. And meaning it.

She intrigued him. She refused to be pigeon-holed. He thought she would stay in his mind. Certainly, he wanted to find out more about her. At twenty-five, it seemed as if she was waiting to grow up.

His silence she took as evidence that he was bored, and she said so, being Lydia. 'You are bored. The last man who took me out was bored with me. It wasn't that I did not make an effort. I think I tried too hard and though what he wanted was delicate sympathy and agreement, what he got were home truths about himself.'

'Poor devil,' he said perfunctorily. 'But you are not boring me. If you stay in that house, though, *you* may be bored.'

'Disappointed,' she corrected.

'Have you never been in love, Lydia?'

'I thought I was in love, sometimes. I always recognized it wasn't love. Just as well,' she said, almost briskly. 'It never does to settle for the second-rate.' I only met this man yesterday and here I am confiding in him, putting my cards on the table, she thought. He was saying he was sure she had the ability to make people like her.

She said grimly, 'I have to work damn hard with some.' For a moment the ghost of Vida hovered.

'People must find you gentle and very kind,' he said. 'I think that is your word and it isn't today's word, is it? *Gentle*. But

145

I think it is what draws people to you.'

What she said next made him stare at her, disconcerted. 'My mother told you it wouldn't work, she told you—asked you—to come here and to take me out, maybe take the sting out of feeling unwanted. To dine me and wine me, as they say, and make me feel attractive. Isn't that so? She has done it before.'

He could have wrung Syb Farmer's neck. He said, 'She asked me if I was passing, to drop in. After all, I have an uncle hereabouts.' But Lydia didn't laugh. He went on, 'Of course she didn't ask me to take you out for the reason you gave. Of course not.' He could do nothing but lie, and a time was to come when bitterly he would regret lying, but now it was all he could do.

How, for God's sake, tell her it was what Syb had said. *Give Lydia a whirl.* If Lydia did suspect it was true she would retreat farther into herself and it was time, he thought, she left the ivory tower and faced life.

'When I marry,' he heard her say, 'I want it to last. Not like Syb and Toby.'

'You marriage will last because you will work at it. Last for ever,' he said. 'I can see

146

the announcement in *The Times.* Golden Wedding.'

She smiled as though he had given her a present.

Next day he drove her up to the hills, the next day to the coast. He took her out every day he was there. She learned about his job and his firm, his ambitions and his leisure time. He liked his job and said flatly that if this were not so he would give it up. 'I have dreams,' he said, 'of leaving London, though. I don't think I could live there for ever. I should like to work in a country town. I should be the newcomer but my children would be born there and grow up and maybe marry and settle down there. One of these English country towns,' he said again. 'Would you like a house there, Lydia?'

'I own two houses now. A third would make me feel like an estate agent.'

He was vaguely disappointed she did not take him seriously enough.

8

'Well, you certainly kept Alec Bartlow to
yourself, Lydia,' Vida said, next day. 'Dull,
I thought him.' Then she said that since
Lydia had come home so late, the night
before, Vida had no chance to tell her
there had been two telephone calls for
her. (I could buy you a little pad to
put beside the telephone, Lydia thought.
With a horrid imitation leather cover, and
a pencil attached. But I won't.)

One call was from Amalie, the other
from Mrs Ellworthy.

'She would not tell me what it was
about,' Vida grumbled. 'I have never cared
for her. She puts on airs. The Colonel's
Lady. Give me Judy O'Grady, any day.'
Which wasn't true.

When Lydia telephoned, Mrs Ellworthy
invited her there to dinner.

'She might have asked the rest of us,'
Vida said.

The Ellworthys were leaving next month.
'I may come here myself,' Lydia said. 'Do

149

that,' she was told. 'It's a house that will suit you.' And get away from that viper, Vida, Mrs Ellworthy thought.

When Lydia returned, Vida was waiting up, this time. That is what she said though it was only ten o'clock. 'I know what she had to tell you,' she crowed. 'They are leaving. I can't think why she didn't tell me when she phoned. But I'm not sorry. We might have been close friends, she and I. I tried. But there was no response. As I said, a snob, stuck-up. Miss Cary was here to collect for the orphanage. Did I tell you, Lydia, that your father and I had an argument about charity? He told me Syb was so generous. I had to tell him I was just as generous within my limits.'

'It's the thought that counts,' Lydia said.

'Yes. Anyway, Miss Cary knew they were leaving. Mrs Ellworthy is on the committee for the orphanage. It is always the same,' Vida said. 'People are newcomers but they push themselves forward. Lydia, what will you do about the house? Lydia,' she said. 'I hope you know how fortunate you are to own two houses?'

'Yes.'

'I have a friend who is looking about

150

here for a house,' Vida said, and went on to describe her friend with the embroidery Lydia had come to expect, and to shut her mind and ears to it if she could. She did hear Vida say, 'In school we were very close. They called us The Terrible Twins. We look alike—'

When she had taken this in, Lydia made her decision. Vida at the bottom of the hill was bad enough, her counterpart at the top was not to be thought of. But not wishing to bring Vida's wrath upon her at the moment, she said, perhaps weakly, she would think about it.

Vida bridled. She was dying to get in touch with her friend and say there was a place ready for her. 'Of course, it's up to you. It is your house to do as you like with, and I am sure that is what you will do. But let me tell you, Daphne is a dear person, jolly, friendly, not like Mrs Ellworthy. Don't come running to me if you refuse Daphne and end up with someone unsuitable. Don't say I didn't try to help.'

Mercifully at that moment the phone bell rang. It was Amalie who seemingly never gave up trying. She invited Lydia up to town and this time Lydia said yes, feeling that anywhere away from Vida for a day or two was what she needed. Amalie was delighted. 'Duke will meet you. It is his free afternoon. He has nothing else to do.'

Lydia was surprised at the pleasure she felt when she saw Duke there beyond the barrier at the station. He smiled broadly. He was muffled against the wind in a long scarf erratically striped. He said a little girl had knitted it for him. 'The daughter of friends of mine. She was a little girl when she started it but she was winning cups for show jumping when she finished.'

'But she stuck at it and did finish. She must like you very much.'

On the way to the flat Lydia asked after Mrs Matthews. Duke said Cherry wasn't too well when he saw her last. 'Lot of 'flu about. The kids flourish, though.'

'Who would look after her if she had 'flu?' Lydia asked. Duke didn't know.

When they reached the block of flats where Amalie lived, turned into the corridor and started walking towards Amalie's front door, there, his back to the door, was a small figure. All he seemed to lack was the begging bowl. When he saw Duke he stood up. It was Will.

'First I went to where you work,' he said, without preamble. 'They said you were off. So I came here. I've only just come. This minute. But I sat down in case you took a long time.' You were certainly filled in with detail if Will had his way. Then he turned to Lydia and smiled his knock-out smile. He took off his woolly glove and held out his hand. 'William Matthews.'

Lydia shook the proffered hand. 'Lydia Farmer.'

'What's wrong?' Duke asked. 'Is it your mother?'

''Flu. So's our neighbour got 'flu. There is no one to give a hand and Ma looks bad. I came to you.'

Duke turned towards Lydia. So did Will. And Lydia took charge. She felt exhilaration sweep through her. Here was something she could do.

First they went into the flat. 'We were here at Christmas,' Will said. 'I know,' Lydia told him. 'I think it was a jolly good thing.'

Will beamed.

Lydia scribbled a note for Amalie. 'The most astonishing thing—I have met a friend I last saw in Monte Video. The husband is an important business man.

Something like Geraint. She is just passing through London and I am going for drinks. Back for dinner. Don't prepare anything. I am taking you to the Savoy. Looking forward to seeing you L.F.'

'What about you?' she asked Duke. 'How do we fit you in?' She had given him the note to read.

'I'll stay with Cherry,' he said promptly, 'when you come back here. I shall have met someone in a pub, someone I knew from way back. Amalie won't want me at the Savoy.'

'Pity.'

In the taxi Will was impressed to hear Lydia's last port of call, so to speak, had been Cape Town. 'Tell me about it,' he said. 'Please. But not at the moment. I just love riding in taxis.'

Cherry was up when she should have been in bed. If you feel as bad as you look, Lydia thought, you feel terrible. Cherry's hair hung round her face. There were shadows beneath her eyes. She looked at them as if she could scarcely see them. She looked like a waif that had been left outside too long. She was trying to cook a stew.

Duke introduced Lydia as a friend.

154

And Cherry, smiling wanly, wept inside. Another elegant woman, smart, smiling, capable looking. A pretty woman, prettier than Amalie. But to Cherry, who loved this man, there did indeed seem to be a stream of elegant women ready to accompany him or live with him.

What can he see in me? Especially today. 'You shouldn't have fetched him,' she told Will. 'Who else?' he said.

'Bed, love,' Lydia said gently, propelling Cherry towards the bedroom. Cherry put up no resistance but did say to Will, 'You said you were going to the museum.'

'You shouldn't have believed me,' Will said.

Lydia fell in love with Lucy and told Will she was relying on him. 'To do what?' he asked with more than a grain of suspicion.

'To tell me where everything is.'

'You staying, then?'

'I'll be here as much as I can.'

'Ma wants someone with her all the time,' Will said but he was looking at Duke. He and Duke went out to shop. Lucy played with her doll's house. Lydia thought her adorable, could hardly take her eyes off her. She lightly brushed with her

155

hand the yellow curls. 'Hallo, Moppet—'

'Lucy,' Lucy said. 'But Moppet if you like.'

When Will and Duke returned, Lydia told him what she planned. With Will out of earshot, she said, 'We will share the burden but don't let Cherry hear us speak the word. I'll organize supper for the children, then go back to Amalie. You stay here and see they get to bed. Can you be with your old school chum that long?'

'Amalie won't miss me.'

More fool her, then, she thought.

When Lydia had finished, she kissed Cherry, and promised to return when she could. When Cherry tried to thank her, Lydia said, 'I enjoyed it.' And meant what she said. She waved to Will, smiled at Cherry, picked Lucy up and half smothered her in kisses, and left. 'I like that lady,' Lucy said.

When they were alone, Duke explained who Lydia was. 'But I don't think she is enjoying it at home as much as she hoped she would. They don't need her.' Cherry said that was an awful thing. And smiled at him. She needed him. She supposed he knew it. Sometimes, when she was separated from him, she tried to be what she called sensible. She tried to turn her thoughts resolutely away from him. A good long word which made no difference at all. Her thoughts nipped round a corner and were back before she had time to spell the word.

Lydia arrived at Amalie's flat with an armful of roses and a string of pretty apologies. Amalie was charmed by it all. After all, few people bothered to charm her. And maybe Lydia might have had more than a modicum of her mother's acting ability for she acted to the life the part of one of the Beautiful People. 'My friend is Swedish,' she elaborated. 'So beautiful. You know what exquisite bones they have. Garbo-esque. Her father was a Swedish millionaire. Timber, you know. But that,' Lydia said, 'is enough about Ingrid. I had to tear myself away but here I am, and it is so kind of you to have me. Such a charming flat,' Lydia said. 'And no staff, of course? But then, a good secretary is a good organizer. Where did I hear that said. Was it Geraint?' She sounded playful. Amalie looked besotted. 'Do you know,' Lydia prattled, 'we might even have discussed you, he and I, in South Africa. He may have said what a splendid secretary he had and I may have said, "Have you?"' Dear God, she thought, forgive me. But she swept Amalie along on a wave of gush and, sweetly, Amalie drowned.

Lydia stunned her with the dress she wore for a meal at the Savoy. A dress that floated as she walked, hand-painted panels of silk. And the diamonds, of course. Amalie did her best and came a poor second, but for once did not mind. She had a glimpse of Paradise, that night. Lydia name-dropped like snowflakes falling. She was depressed rather to find how easy it was. She raked through people who had stayed at hotels where she had stayed, if only for a night.

Amalie lapped it all up. She was a grateful, responsive guest.

Halfway through the meal Lydia was tired of looking at her.

You are not the woman for him. Oh no, Lydia thought, not Duke. He must marry little Mrs Matthews. At the thought of Duke and Cherry, Will and Lucy, living happily ever after, she beamed on Amalie. Then enquired after Duke. Amalie shrugged. 'Like you, he met an old school friend. Out of the blue. I think Duke is

158

shy,' Amalie said, frowning, sounding as if it were a disease. 'He needn't be. He is a public school man, you know. And Oxford. When I think of that background—'

Lydia looked at her plate.

But when they reached home Duke was there. Amalie, who was very happy, said that supper at the Savoy did something for you. Duke agreed and told them his mother used to say the same about tea at the Ritz after an afternoon's shopping. She said it soothed her no end. Amalie looked at him to see if he was taking the mickey. He is not, Lydia thought. I might. He isn't.

'Do you have to go back tomorrow evening?' Amalie asked her. 'I can't think what there is at Vida's place to make you want to go back.'

'I may go on to Scotland. I shall pick up a few things,' Lydia said.

Amalie had arranged to take the next day off from work. Duke went out early before they were up. Lydia knew why. He was going round to Cherry's to find out how she was before going to work. Lydia herself would go there when she was supposed to be on her way back home. But before she left London she took Amalie shopping. She made Amalie a present of a dress Amalie coveted, giving it to her with the right amount of careless indifference used by a young woman to whom money was no obstacle in getting what she wanted. Amalie was almost speechless with gratitude. When they arrived home, there was a phone call for Lydia. It was Alec.

'I telephoned you at the house,' he said. 'They told me you were in London. Are you staying long? You promised you would get in touch. I thought we might go to a theatre.'

There was silence. 'Hallo?' she heard him say. 'Does it need all that much thinking about?'

'May I make you an accessory, not to crime, exactly, but to subterfuge?' she said. 'I am pretending to go back tonight.' (Just as well, she thought, Amalie had urged her to take the call in Amalie's bedroom.) 'So please don't telephone me there again. Not this week.'

'I see,' he said, the voice still charming, still friendly. But the mind colder than usual with regard to this girl. He thought he saw. Another girl would say openly she was off with a man for a few days, which

160

Alec decided was what she meant. Not this one. She had to bury it in mystery that would do credit to a Victorian. 'Have fun,' he said and rang off.

Lydia did not recognize coolness. Her mind was fixed on one thing, helping the Matthews family. Alec Bartlow could wait. She forgot about him.

She bade Amalie goodbye, said what fun it had been, said insincerely they must do it again some day when Lydia had shopping to do. She said it with just the right amount of indifference to any detailed planning that made it impossible for Amalie to say, 'But when?'

When Lydia arrived at Cherry's flat Duke was there. He said, 'I'll go back now. I can't keep on meeting old school pals. Lydia, what if Amalie telephones Vida to ask after you?'

'I said I might be going to Scotland. Go on from there. Tell her to be her age. Ask her if she thinks I would be going to Scotland on my own. Ask her to keep it from Vida. Try to make it sound like a scion of the jet set.' Then she apologized. Her manners were not as good as his.

Cherry looked better. Her hair was tied back with cherry-coloured ribbon. 'Duke fetched it,' she said. The children came in to say their prayers and to say goodnight. Duke had given them supper. 'Do I have to go to bed when Lucy goes?' Will said.

Cherry said no. He might read a book for some time longer. 'You never,' he told Lydia, 'get anything unless you ask.'

'Does he sound big-headed to you?' Cherry asked when Will had gone.

'Perhaps surprisingly, no.'

Cherry said she was glad. Lydia made a mound of scrambled egg, light and fluffy, made toast and tea. Cherry ate her supper luxuriating against pillows. Lydia sat in a chair with a plate on her lap. Will, eating a second supper at Lydia's invitation, ate at the kitchen table and read from a book propped up in front of him. He thought this wonderfully adult but even he was tired at last and went to bed.

When they were alone, Lydia said, 'If you talk about him, which of course is what you want to do, will it make you cry?'

'No. I'm in love with him. Or I love him. Who couldn't love him? I think he is one of the best people I have met. He's different from Bert,' Cherry said and smiled. 'Bert was young, we were

162

both daffy in those days. I loved Bert too. I shall always love him. But I'm not the girl who fell in love with Bert any more. Bert was a tough-looking boy. Stocky. Dark with a bandit moustache. And a heart as soft as marshmallow. He was so proud of Will. I think he wanted Will to inherit the earth.'

'Will will have a good try.'

'Yes,' Cherry said, 'he was different, Bert, from this man. But Bert would have liked him. He would have said he was a good fella.'

The rest of the week passed quickly and happily for Lydia while she nursed Cherry and bossed the children for their own good. She took them shopping and pretended they were hers. It was a lovely feeling. At the end of the week she took them all to Brighton where she had booked them in at a hotel for a fortnight. She had already discussed her plan of campaign with Cherry which was that when the Ellworthys left, Cherry would move into the house. 'Housekeep for me,' Lydia said. 'You will like it there. The sea is near. Nice hills and walks.'

'Will you move up the hill?'

'I may.'

Driven into it, Cherry told herself. Lydia had let slip a little of what it was like at Vida's. Cherry filled in with what Lydia did not say. She knew Lydia's first enthusiasm was dribbing out like sawdust from a doll.

And Cherry was furious, wondering how they could treat thus anyone so filled with love. Too much love, Cherry thought. When there is no one to accept it, it turns in on itself and shrivels and dies. Worse, it can fester. She didn't think this would happen to Lydia. But the love would die, no doubt about that.

But with Cherry and Will and Lucy, Lydia was a changed person. No need here to be on the defensive, always to explain what you meant, to say where you were going and why. No need here to pretend. They were uncomplicated and likeable and they loved her. Without undue conceit, she knew they did. Even Will. Lucy, of course, she adored.

For the first time, in this small flat, she knew what home was. The idea, the concept, she told herself, was worth pursuing. Even if she had drawn blank with Toby and Vida, she must go on looking for it. Otherwise there was no life for her.

Vida, it transpired, had characteristically taken no notice of what Lydia said but took it upon herself to offer the house to her friend Daphne. 'It will be quite all right. Lydia is just being difficult. But she will say yes if I tell her to. It will be wonderful, Daph, for us to be close again.'

She was furious when she knew of Lydia's plans. 'I have as good as told Daphne she can come.'

Syb would have said, 'You had no business to. Now tell her she can't come.' Lydia only said a friend of hers was coming here from London.

'I didn't know you had any friends,' Vida said rudely. When Lydia explained, 'Children?' she screeched. 'Daphne has no children. Just the two of them. Daphne is as house proud as I am. Children will wreck the place. But it serves you right. What am I going to tell Daphne?' she appealed to Ellie who was listening.

'That you jumped the gun,' Ellie said. 'I told you to wait until Lydia came back.'

When Lydia left the room, Ellie followed her.

9

'I want to leave home,' Ellie said baldly. She asked Lydia if she would stake her while she looked for a job and somewhere to live. 'If you mean to shower me with birthday and Christmas presents for the next couple of years,' Ellie said brazenly, 'you might lump them together and give me the cash. You can afford it and I must get away from here. I can't stand it. Pa doesn't care and Ma smothers me.'

'You wouldn't go without her knowing?'

'It's the only way I shall go. She never wants anyone to leave. This is her kingdom, you know that, and anyone who wants to leave is a traitor. *God Bless Our Happy Home,*' Ellie said. 'And I believe she thinks it is happy. Maybe it would do her good—jolt her—if someone did leave. Pa is snug. So is Ben. It's up to me to make a break.'

'She will be hurt if you run away.'

'She will be bloody furious but it's my life.'

Lydia was silent. She thought she knew what mind picture enchanted Ellie when she thought of life in the big city, fun galore, a job a necessary evil to provide the goodies which were there in abundance. Ellie would fall for the silly fringe, burning up youth and looks and good sense as well as burning her fingers. Whatever Ellie thought herself, to Lydia she appeared irresponsible, far removed from the image of a girl who could look after herself for the best in London.

'You mean you won't help?' Ellie said.

'You must tell your mother.'

Bitterly disappointed, Ellie turned and ran from the room, colliding with Vida who was entering with an armful of fresh linen. Ellie did not stop to help pick up the sheets and pillow-cases. Lydia did it for her.

'What have you been saying to Ellie?' Vida asked.

'I gave her what I think is good advice.'

'When she needs advice, she can come to me.'

'That is what I told her.'

But when, later, Vida asked Ellie what it was she had spoken to Lydia about, Ellie, resentful and smarting, concocted a lie to make what mischief she could. 'Oh, Lydia is on to me to leave home. She says I ought to go to London to work. She says I shouldn't stay here. I shall get nowhere. Besides, London is where the fun is.'

'*Leave home?*'

'She says there are plenty of jobs in London.'

'Maybe,' Vida said. 'But you are all right where you are.' She did not directly confront Lydia with this evidence of treachery, which is what she called it, and which Ellie knew she would call it. She told Toby about it, greatly incensed. But he said it might be a good thing if Ellie left home. Thousands of girls did it.

'You don't want to lose your second daughter?' Vida said.

Toby shrugged, his way of saying he wouldn't mind.

But next day, Ellie was back wheedling Lydia. 'Have you thought it over—what I said?'

'I've told you. I will help you, but not to run away.'

'Oh, all right.' Then Ellie said, 'Come to a party, tonight. One of the gang, Johnny, has a birthday. You are stuck here, night after night. You will grow old before your time.'

'Shan't I be too old for the party?'

Ellie shrugged. 'If you come, you can give me a lift there.'

'What about a lift back?'

'You *are* old before your time! We'll see about that later.'

Lydia, while having no desire to go to the party, since she was sure her ideas of parties and Ellie's were poles apart, thought she might as well go so that she might see for herself the sort of person Ellie went around with. From hints Ellie dropped, Lydia was certain Vida would not approve.

And what Ellie wanted was for Lydia to see at first hand the gang in action. When they got going, they were hard to stop, Ellie told herself, and Lydia might easily be shocked. She might say, 'Little sister, I had no idea. We must get you away at once before you are corrupted further. How much money do you want?'

'Wear the outfit you wore the first night here,' Ellie said. She said it deliberately for, still smarting under Lydia's refusal, she didn't mind if Lydia looked like a sore thumb—her words. Lydia would look absurd in her long skirt and white blouse, with her neat hair and silver earrings, in what was to be a jeans and pants party, a scruffy party, a party of stupid girls and stupider boys.

Lydia's heart sank when she stood in the doorway and took in the scene. Ellie, introducing her to no one, left immediately. Lydia sat on a sofa and felt like Jane Eyre at her most governessy.

The room pulsed with noise. There was occasionally the sound of breaking glass and the shriek and the laugh that goes with it. The music seemed to Lydia to jump off the walls on to her head and to thump there. There was plenty of cheap drink but empty plates gave evidence that the food was all used up and no one was going to replace it.

She eyed the guests and thought morosely most of them would be better for being thrown out into the air, hosed down and sent home. Long-haired girls and long-haired boys. Hard to tell them apart. I am getting old, she thought. But not old before my time. If this is eighteen I am quite willing to be twenty-five.

She remembered herself at eighteen, just left school, ready for the strict discipline

171

of the Swiss finishing school she was sent to.

She thought of Duke and of Alec, and wondered what they would think if they could see her now. Duke would be kind. Alec would ask her what the hell she thought she was doing here. They would both take her home.

I am no Puritan. I have been to parties, in my time, some of them hectic. This is just a cheap common do. They are a cheap lot. Where would they be at her age? She hoped some would have given up this sort of thing. Occasionally the language she heard made her sick. There was something about the use of dirty language by her own sex that turned her stomach.

Then why stay? There was no need to stay. No one asked her if she was enjoying herself. It wasn't that sort of party. Good manners went out with clean necks. She decided to go home and to take Ellie with her. She stood up but was furious when she found herself pushed back down and eyed belligerently by a lanky, sallow youth with hair over his neck and beady black eyes. Truculently drunk. And not prepossessing, she thought. Definitely not. He sat beside her, pushed his face close to hers, and said, 'You know what you are?'

'A stuck-up bitch, yes.'

'Where did you get that accent?'

'Not here.'

'Coming here, slumming—' he accused.

'Yes,' she said. 'I am a bit long in the tooth too.'

He said offensively, 'I don't mind 'em old.' Then he came back to the present and to her. 'Not going. Not yet.'

'I am going now.'

'Who did you come with?'

'Ellie Farmer. I'm her sister.'

'Half sister,' he corrected, showing he knew the family history. 'The one with the lolly—'

'That's right.' He smelled of drink and Lydia made a face at him. He saw it and made to hit her. She pushed him. The drink he held slopped over his shirt. He lifted his hand again. She caught it with her left hand and smacked his face with her right.

'I hate stuck up bitches,' he breathed.

'And I loathe you.'

'I'll kill you—'

'Oh, turn it off,' she snapped in language he might understand. 'You're a pig and repulsive. What are you? A repulsive pig. Where is Ellie?'

'Upstairs, I suppose. And she won't want to go home. Not our Ellie. School is out for her when she leaves mama—'

Lydia told him to shut up, smacked the other side of the pimply face for good measure, rose and went to the door. He looked after her, swearing.

Lydia went out into the hall. If necessary, though she hoped it would not be necessary since the last thing she wished to do was traipse through the place, she would search room by room for Ellie. She could imagine what she would find. But Ellie stood at the top of the stairs, apparently waiting for Lydia. When she saw her she ran down and clutched her. 'I want to go home.'

And you, Lydia thought, are a rotten actress. This was what she told Ellie later in the kitchen where Lydia made tea and scrubbed her face under the kitchen tap, scrubbed her hands clean as if she meant to get off every trace even of the air she might have been polluted with.

'That,' Lydia said, 'was for my benefit, wasn't it? Not the Zoo. That, God help us, was for real. But I was to go there, be shaken by what I saw, and think you

174

should be helped to leave.'

Ellie didn't deny it. She only flared, 'It's all right for you. You can meet the right people, and if you don't like them you can go somewhere else. This house is like a prison. I'll never get out, never—'

'If you scream,' Lydia said, 'I'll smack you like I smacked him.'

'Who did you smack? Lydia, who did you smack?'

'We weren't introduced.' But Lydia described him. Ellie groaned. 'My God, that was Johnny. It was his party.'

There is a first time for everything. Lydia had never before been to a party where she smacked her host's face. Ellie, disappointed and tired, put her head on her arms and wept.

'I'll give you the money if you tell your mother,' Lydia said.

Ellie wept harder. A wonder Vida did not hear and come down and blame Lydia.

Next day, Saturday, Lydia met Alec again. He met her walking back from the village. 'She has walked there,' Vida told him when he called at the house. 'I can't think why. Nothing would do but she must buy a car for herself. Now she has a car, she walks.'

'I'll walk to meet her,' he said.

The smile Lydia gave him when she recognized him was radiant, so radiant he remarked on it so she asked him if people did not usually smile when they met him. 'Not always at such strength.'

'What are you doing here?'

'I wanted to get out of London for the weekend. They said the weather would be good. And I can't get you out of my mind.' He hadn't meant to say it. It was out before he could stop himself.

Her eyes danced. 'In a romantic novel, that must come near the end. It would be something of A Declaration. But this isn't a romantic novel. So it must be brotherly concern. Thank you.'

If she but knew, he had never felt brotherly concern for a pretty girl in his life. He asked her if she had enjoyed herself wherever she went.

'Brighton? Oh yes.'

Brighton. He didn't believe it. Nothing so hackneyed 'Though I was only there for a day or two—'

'But I thought—'

'I spent the rest of the week in Fulham.'

'You're having me on!'

'I'm telling the truth.' She told him the story then. 'Lies, deceit,' she said happily. 'A tangled web. If it catches up with me I shall be sunk. But I enjoyed every minute of it. You should meet Lucy. Better still, you should wait until she grows up and then marry her for she is both lovely and well mannered.'

She really has enjoyed herself, he thought. It was what she wanted. To be involved, to make people happy, to try to solve their problems for them. 'Cherry and Will and Lucy are coming to live here,' she said. 'When you get a week's leave, if you care to, spend it there. Cherry will look after you.'

'Do you plan to live there yourself?'

'If I'm kicked out,' she said cheerfully. He thought the Matthews family were good for her.

'I suppose,' Vida said, a few evenings later, 'men have chased you for your money, Lydia?'

'You can always tell.'

'*How?*'

'When they speak of love they have a dollar sign in both eyes.'

Vida snuffed. 'The Ellworthys leave tomorrow.'

'Yes. They are dining with me tonight at The George.'

This incensed Vida greatly. 'Why not here? Are you ashamed of asking them here? I know it isn't what you have been accustomed to but it is your home. You should have asked them here. It is your home,' Vida repeated.

There was no answer to this so Lydia excused herself and left the room, leaving Vida fuming.

When Ben came in she said, after complaining that the Ellworthys, whom she cordially disliked, were not dining here that night, their last night. 'Ben, I shouldn't be surprised if you had Lydia in the family.'

'Alec, you mean? Perhaps. They look rather good together,' Ben said.

Vida snapped that they were not sitting for their portrait.

Cherry Matthews was delighted when she saw what was to be their home. 'When are you coming here? You can't stay a lodger down there when you might be here.'

'Châteleine? Mistress of the place? I don't know if I am cut out for that—'

'I know what you are cut out for,' Cherry said. 'A husband and a home of your own and kids like Will and Lucy.'

'I should adore Lucy but could I cope with Will?' Lydia was giving nothing away, her smile and her voice were light. 'To paraphrase Mrs Beeton, if she did say the original, "First catch your man".'

Later, when Cherry saw Alec and Lydia together, she knew that the man was caught.

But now she returned to the question that was usually in the front of her mind. When would she see Duke again? Would he visit here? If he did, it wasn't a very tall hill. With his strides he could be at the top in no time at all.

10

Vida left to spend ten days with an aged aunt in Tunbridge Wells. There were, Vida hinted, 'expectations'. Toby left to play golf in Wales.

Ben, Lydia and Ellie were together in the house.

The morning Lydia discovered fifty pounds was missing from a drawer in her room she also discovered Ellie had decamped, leaving a note on the kitchen table. 'I am off to London. I've packed in my job. I have a friend I can stay with and if I find a job no one can make me come back. Be a sport—don't tell Ma, not until she comes back.'

When Lydia told Ben he only said, vaguely, 'A week in London will do the child good.'

Had Ellie taken the fifty pounds? Lydia was afraid this was so. Ellie had been in the room when Lydia had put the notes in the drawer, had commented, 'What's that? Pocket money?'

After breakfast, Lydia drove to Wadden to the office where Ellie worked. She had met Ellie's friend, Sandra. Sandra was receptionist so it was easy for Lydia to ask her to lunch at a nearby restaurant. Sandra, over the meal, was prepared to tell all, not being the most loyal of friends.

'Ellie handed in her notice yesterday. Mr Byers took it. Between you and me, I think he was glad to. Ellie isn't the world's keenest. Wastes her time, comes late. She used to meet Johnny, some lunchtimes, then she was late coming back. The trouble is Ellie thinks the place isn't good enough for her. You were at the party, weren't you? You met Johnny?'

Lydia could only nod. She decided not to say she had smacked his face and called him a pig.

'Johnny broke his guitar over a chap's head,' Sandra said and giggled. 'Did you see it? Johnny has an awful temper.'

'I had left then.'

'Oh, pity.' For a time Sandra applied herself to the meal. For sweet, she had a double portion of ice cream with nuts and chocolate sauce. 'I'm always saying I mean to diet but I never do. Anyway, to get back to Ellie. She is keen on Johnny. Or on his

Lotus, more like. Johnny is spoiled rotten. I don't think his people know what to do with him. I think the Lotus and so on are Danegeld,' Sandra said and giggled again.

'Ellie hasn't gone off with him?'

'No fear. He wouldn't take her,' Sandra said spitefully. 'No. If she's with anyone she is with Paula. Paula West. Paula used to work at the office but she left. She lives in Putney. Shares a flat with two girls, she was telling me at Christmas. Paula says it's smashing. Freedom and all that. I'm going as soon as I get the chance. I don't suppose Paula will want Ellie there but she will have to do more than hint before Ellie leaves. That girl has a thick skin. I don't know where Ellie got the money from. Was it from you? She said she was going to tap you for it.'

'I didn't give it to her.'

'Oh well. Good luck to her. You going after her? She won't thank you.' Sandra never did say thank you for the lunch.

Lydia, back in the house, telephoned. Alec Bartlow in London. A secretary with a silk-smooth voice put her through to him. 'This is the wrong way round,' said

183

the honest Lydia, 'but can you meet me after work?'

He laughed and her spirits lightened. It had been a miserable day, up to now. She said, 'You are free, this evening?'

'I am. What's the problem? There must be one. You're not the sort of girl, more's the pity, to phone me in office time if there isn't something wrong. Out with it.'

'How well you know me. I always think I'm being a nuisance. I have a run-away sister, half-sister. I want to find her and bring her back.'

'Sound like an old movie, a real classic. *Lost in London,*'

'Oh, I know where she is—'

'But you want support? I'm flattered it's me. Though I should prefer an evening with you without your runaway sister. Still, half a load—'

She had to say it. 'Or half a sister—'

'I think,' said silky-voice to a colleague later, 'that our Mr Bartlow has a lady at last. And about time. I had thought about him myself. But he seemed stubborn and I couldn't really bother. I wonder who she is and what she's like.'

'What did she sound like?'

'Strangely enough, like the boss's wife.'

184

When they met it took Alec a little time to get out of Lydia the story of the theft as well as the run-away. 'My fault,' she sighed. 'I should have locked it away.'

'You weren't to know there were magpies around! Don't you think it would be better for her to come here, away from Johnny and the rest?'

'Yes. But not without telling her mother. It would really upset Vida if Ellie went without letting her know.'

He wondered if Vida would be as considerate of Lydia's feelings.

They knocked at the door of the address Sandra had given. A girl answered the knock, a girl who, this time of day, looked tired. A working girl in London can look tired at six o'clock in the evening. It was something Ellie hadn't thought of. When Lydia explained who she was, Paula asked her in, then called, 'Friends to see you, Ellie.'

Paula had not been too pleased when Ellie had presented herself at the door. 'Surprise, surprise,' Ellie had trilled, adding, as she would, those awful words, 'Long time no see. You going to work? Can I come in. I'll sleep on the floor.'

'What are you doing in London?'

'Come to look it over. What is it like for jobs? I've packed it in with old Byers.'

'You won't find the streets paved with gold,' Paula had said. She supposed she had to let Ellie in but if Ellie stayed she was going to pay her share. Sleep on the floor, but pay for it. No scrounging. But knowing Ellie she had to ask where Ellie had got the money from to come here. 'My rich step-sister loaned me fifty pounds.'

'That won't go far.'

Alec and Lydia glimpsed Ellie before she saw them. Ellie was standing in front of a mirror, trying on clothes. She wore a black coat to her ankles and a floppy-brimmed, black felt hat. Alec thought she looked like a professional mourner, especially with the mauve feather boa tossed round her neck.

'Nanny's here, love,' Paula said.

But when she saw the despairing look on Ellie's face as Ellie turned and stared at Alec and Lydia, Paula's heart softened. She immediately associated the newcomers with Them and the opposition. She said, instinctively, 'You don't have to go back, Ellie. You can stay here.'

Ellie looked at Lydia. Lydia said nothing. Ellie, perhaps thinking of the fifty pounds, reddened.

'Come on,' Alec said. 'Where's your case? Give it to me and I'll take it to the car.'

Paula thought Ellie looked as if she was walking away between gaolers.

In the car on the way home Lydia let Ellie rave on about the injustices of life. 'You have so much! You own this and own that. Shares, dividends, property. Money rolls in—'

'Not quite as you describe it. You make me sound like an oil sheikh. There are such things as taxes.'

'Taxes, hell. You never look as though you are deprived of much. Why couldn't I have a bit? You haven't mentioned it but I did take fifty pounds. It would take me weeks to save fifty pounds.'

'If you had asked, I would have given it to you.'

Ellie said sullenly, 'I've asked until I'm sick.'

'And I've told you. You can't just run away. You have to tell your parents. Ellie,' Lydia said patiently, 'you know your mother would race up to London or wherever you were to tell you to come back.'

'Well, *you* didn't have to.' She sounded what she was. A spoiled child.

'Do it properly when you go,' Lydia urged. 'A job to go to. A place to stay.'

Next day, of course, Ellie had no job to go to. This did not seem to worry her. She slept until lunch time, mooned around the house all afternoon, stayed out until well after midnight. Lydia found she could not get off to sleep until Ellie was back. Toby extended his golfing holiday, Vida was doing her duty in Tunbridge Wells. 'No,' she had told Lydia when she telephoned and Lydia said she hoped Vida was enjoying herself. 'No, I can't say that it is a holiday. My aunt is old and tiresome, an exacting woman. But it is my duty to visit her to show her she is not forgotten. And I hope I shall always know where my duty lies.'

Alec Bartlow had telephoned twice. The first time the day after the rescue of Ellie, to ask how things were, and the second time to tell Lydia he was leaving for France and Italy. 'On the job—' he emphasized as men are quick to do. When he came back, he would, if she still wanted him, take her up on her offer to stay at the house on the hill. 'Do that—' she said, and her tranquil tone annoyed him somewhat. He could wish she sounded more enthusiastic.

There were two nights to go before Vida was due back.

I shan't tell her a thing, Lydia thought. But I am going to ask Toby to do something for Ellie. One keeps forgetting Toby which is what he hopes for. If my father could fade into the pattern of the wall paper he would be delighted.

I shall offer to help financially with Ellie if he needs it. He can tell Vida or not, as he pleases. But Ellie can't go on like this. Something will happen to her.

That night, it did, and it was mild compared with what might have happened.

Ellie came home at two o'clock in the morning. When Lydia saw the state she was in, she was horrified but bit back questioning. There was a swelling around Ellie's eye which tomorrow would be a black eye and a beauty. Bruises on her neck and scratches on her face. Her stockings were in shreds, her knees and legs grazed and bloodied. She had lost her shoes.

She stared at Lydia, then started to cry. Lydia helped her into the kitchen, seated her in the chair, bathed and saw to the cuts. All the time silence except for Ellie's shuddering sobs. But the sobs lessened. *'Nothing happened,'* Ellie said. 'I'll tell you that before you ask. *Nothing happened*. Don't think it did.'

'I am not thinking anything.' Lydia made fresh tea. She sat opposite Ellie and waited.

'Suddenly, I was sick of him,' Ellie said. 'He kept pawing me. I know what he wanted. He called me names because he didn't get it. I was sick of him. He was drunk. Then he started to shout. He has an awful temper. I swear he'll kill somebody, one day. At the party, he smashed his guitar over a boy's head.'

'Sandra told me.'

'Oh yes. I forgot you talked to Sandra. Anyway, I pushed him away. I had to fight him off. You haven't got to show Johnny you don't want him. He hit me across the face. We fought. Then he opened the car door and pushed me out. I fell on to the road. I lost my shoes,' Ellie sniffed. 'But I walked home. I'm sick of him, sick of him—' Her own voice rose to a scream.

'I never want to see him again.'

Lydia undressed her and got her to bed, waited until Ellie was asleep. Tomorrow, she thought, Toby is back. I shall have a showdown with him. She blamed herself for not having done this before. She shuddered when she pictured a girl walking along dark country lanes with a lout of a boy somewhere within driving distance.

When Lydia said no, what she wanted to say would not wait but must be said there and then, Toby wished Vida was there. It was inconsiderate of her to stay away longer than he did. Vida usually took it upon herself to face whatever cropped up. She should be here now. Lydia looked stubborn enough. He sighed and wondered what was wrong and what was the easiest way round it. Lydia told him Ellie wanted to leave home. She told him about Ellie running off to London but she made no mention of the fifty pounds. Toby was shrewd when he wished to be. 'Where did she get the money? She never has any. She can't save a penny. Pinched it from you, no doubt,' Toby hazarded. At the sight of Lydia's face he said, 'I thought so. I hope you got it back. Some of it. London is expensive. You are a bit unfairly balanced, you know, you and Ellie,' their father said. 'Financially.'

'Perhaps. There isn't much I can do about it.'

'And Vida keeps her on a tight apron string,' Toby said.

'You've noticed? Why don't you do something about it?'

'You don't know much about the way a family is run, do you? Well, I suppose not,' he conceded. 'Syb and I didn't give you much chance to notice. Not for long. But a man usually leaves his wife to bring up a daughter. Vida has always had her say about Ellie. But if she wants to go to London, why not? The house will be more cheerful without her grizzles. Do you think she can look after herself? Bit of a jungle, I gather, London, these days.'

'I think she will make an effort,' Lydia said. 'And I will stake her.'

Toby said that was good of her, damn decent. Lydia said, 'Will you tell Vida?'

'Why not you?'

'It isn't my place to tell her.'

He sighed. He said, 'Your trouble is that you get too involved with people. You go around poking about for crises to cope with. You are like your mother. Syb couldn't see a cauldron bubble without giving it a stir! I told you before, when you are married you will have troubles of your own. What about Bartlow?'

'He seems to be affianced to an airways schedule.'

'If you've noticed, that's something. For God's sake, get married—' her father said.

'Then we can have some peace—' she finished for him. Fuming, she said she didn't know which she found worse to take, Toby's indifference or his cheek.

'You are not bad looking,' he said.

'A pale copy of my mother.'

Toby was interested. 'Is that what they say? Oh, there is no one like Syb.'

'Why did you divorce her, then?'

'She was beautiful but she was impossible to live with. When we walked into a restaurant, heads used to turn. I felt quite proud of her. But when we got home she was liable to throw something. You are easier to live with.'

As a recommendation it left her cold.

When she told Ellie what Toby said, Lydia went on, 'And I will give you money to start you off. That idea of yours of clubbing together birthday and

Christmas presents, I'll do that—'

Ellie had the grace to look shamefaced. 'Thanks.' There was a pause, then, 'You didn't tell him about the fifty pounds?'

'No.'

'What do I tell Ma tomorrow about my eye—and the rest?'

'Why not tell her the truth?'

'I couldn't. She would be down at Johnny's, ready to brain him. When I was a kid,' Ellie said, 'I used to think it was wonderful—Ma's partisanship, if that is what it is. Whatever you had done, she would stick up for you in front of the others. A right Tartar she sounded. She might give you stick when you got home but she rooted for you outside. As I say, it made me feel well defended. But when I grew up, it somehow became a barrier between learning to grow up, living my own life. It seemed more like interfering.' Another pause, then, 'I would have paid back the fifty pounds, Lydia.'

'Yes.'

Predictably, Vida made a great fuss when she saw the state of Ellie's face, rushing to her, turning the poor face to the light, demanding to be told how it had happened and what they had done in the way of first aid. 'If I'm not here, nothing goes right. I only have to turn my back.'

Ellie said she had fallen, and stuck to her story. Vida berated her for her hoyendish behaviour. 'What were you doing? Climbing a tree? You are too old for that sort of thing. Lydia, where were you?'

'Not up the neighbouring tree.'

'Don't sauce me! You are the older sister. You should have more control over her. You have no idea,' Vida told Ellie, 'how I worry over you, where you go and who you go with. Mothers do worry.'

'Ma, you are giving me a headache.'

'And don't *you* sauce me! Terrible things happen today,' Vida said with truth. 'That boy Johnny. He drives too fast. He drinks. He is a bad lot, Ellie. I forbid you to see him.'

'Yes, Ma.'

'Don't think you have taken me in by this story about climbing trees—'

Ellie waited for the storm to blow itself out. But fortified by her holiday, Vida was on form.

She had plenty of breath left for the next storm which was at the dinner table. Toby told Vida, without preamble, in fact rudely interrupting what she was saying about her aunt's house in Tunbridge Wells, that Ellie would soon be going to London to live and to work.

When she could speak, Vida said no, Ellie was not going.

'As soon as we can get her fixed up,' Toby said, as if Vida had said nothing. 'She must go. She is wasting her time here with the yokels—'

'What a silly word. Some of the girls are quite nice.'

'Wasting her time,' Toby repeated. 'I won't say her talents because I'm not certain about those.'

Listening, Lydia wished he would not tease Ellie. He had a habit of doing it and it came close to the sadistic because Ellie was never able to repay in kind. She sat now glowering at her plate.

'Look at her,' Toby said. 'Half the time I swear she doesn't wash her neck.'

'Of course I wash my neck—'

'Toby,' Vida said, 'the dinner table is not the place to talk about washing one's neck. That is for the bathroom.'

'Well, if we meet in the bathroom, I'll say it again,' Toby teased.

'I'll be glad to get to London,' Ellie said, and Lydia sympathized with her.

'Look at the way she dresses,' Toby went on. 'She wouldn't be out of place in a fairground, taking the money—' He said, 'Compared with Lydia—'

This was enough for Vida. 'Oh yes, compared with Lydia. I am certain Ellie and I cut poor figures, country cousins, frumps, compared with Lydia. We don't have Lydia's money. Nor Lydia's lazy life. Lydia can shop around for what she wants. Ellie has to shop on Saturdays. So don't compare Ellie with Lydia, Toby—'

My God, Lydia thought, it's like a gramophone record. If someone would only lift the needle off.

'At least,' Vida said, 'Ellie has a job.'

'Not any more, Ma. I gave it up.'

Toby cracked a walnut. 'She goes to London, next week.'

'You wormed this out of your father, he is too weak to say no,' Vida accused Ellie. 'When my back was turned.'

'She didn't. I arranged it,' Lydia said.

Vida turned to her. Her cheeks were scarlet. 'What has it got to do with you? What has anything in this house to do with you?'

'It's her house,' Ellie muttered. Even now she could not forbear to take a dig at her mother.

Lydia, fearing for Vida's blood pressure, said, 'I think it's time she left home. Other girls do.'

'What do you know about a home?' Vida shouted. 'You've never had a home. Dragged round from one place to the next—'

'Vida,' Toby said.

'What?'

'Just as well Ben is in bed with a stomach upset.'

'Why?'

'You sound vulgar.'

Vida breathed hard. 'And who will keep Ellie if she does go? Do I? Out of the housekeeping money?'

'Lydia has promised to give me the money,' Ellie said.

Then there was silence, only broken by the aggravating sound of Toby cracking nuts.

At last Vida said, 'I might have guessed.' The red had receded from her face, leaving her looking pale and old. Lydia felt sorry for her but was glad Vida had no way of knowing. 'This has been on your mind since you came. Breaking up the home. I've seen it. I know what is in your mind.'

'Don't be ridiculous,' Toby told her.

'Of course you would stick up for her,' Vida said, without much evidence, so far, to back up her statement. 'But if Ellie goes, Lydia goes. You won't be satisfied,' she told Lydia dramatically, 'until you have done your worst.'

'*Next week, East Lynne*,' Toby said.

'When that letter came, I sensed bad news,' Vida said. 'I thought it was the house you were after. It's the family you want to wreck. You are a wrecker. Like your mother.'

Toby opened his mouth to speak and Vida was all set to say, 'Don't you defend her—' when there was a ring of the door bell.

'I'll go,' Vida said, and figuratively switched off her big scene. She bustled off into the hall.

When she opened the door and saw who was there she stood as if transfixed.

Syb smiled. 'May I come in?'

11

Syb wore a cream wool suit with a large-brimmed cowboy hat of cream felt. Tall, slim, dark, she looked superb. Wordlessly, Vida stood aside to let her in. 'You are at dinner?' Syb said, apologetically. Vida said it didn't matter, which Syb took as an invitation to walk to the door of the dining-room and stand there, smiling. Lydia kissed her. Toby expressed pleasure at the sight of her and kissed her too. She made Ellie feel a bumpkin but there and then Ellie fell in love with Syb or the imagine of Syb, fell down and worshipped it. Syb said, 'My word, that's a shiner! Went slap into a door, I'll be bound.'

'And you, my love,' she asked Lydia. 'How are you? No country roses in your cheeks, yet?'

When Vida asked if Syb had eaten, Syb said yes but she would love coffee. They had coffee in the sitting-room.

Damn good-looking woman still, Toby told himself. But as fidgety as she ever was. She may sit still, if that is what she calls it, but her eyes are never still. They flick here and there, she misses nothing. On someone else they could be described as shifty, I swear. But not Syb.

She was saying to Vida, 'You've changed the old place.' But did not say, 'For the better.'

'And Lydia wants to change it again,' Vida said, her lips thin.

'*Good,*' Syb said. They could take it which way they liked. But she said the coffee was excellent.

Queening it there, Vida fumed, as if she dropped in to give us the benefit of half-an-hour in her presence. She heard Syb say, 'Now give us the news'

'Which of us?' Toby asked.

'I shall start with Lydia.'

'Nothing much to tell,' Lydia said. 'Where are you staying?'

'Where do you suggest?' Syb murmured. She felt happier. There was something in the air here. Conflict. She had interrupted something. She hoped that, despite her presence, they would continue with it.

She had left America on an impulse to see how Lydia was getting on here in England. Was she, she asked herself now, going to be rewarded by finding herself at the heart of a domestic crisis? She hoped so. She heard Lydia invite her mother to the house at the top of the hill. 'I shall be there myself.'

No one else said a word. Be sports, Syb urged, silently. Speak up. Carry on as if I am not here.

Then Ellie said her piece. When she considered it, later, Ellie gave thanks that something had urged her to do this. She wondered if she had recognized a turning point in her life and grabbed it, so to speak? Did she recognize this lovely woman in her cream wool suit as Ellie's *deus ex machina*, and one who might not reappear? 'We are in the middle of a row,' Ellie said.

Syb smiled at her. The child needs doing over. Her skin is spotty but fewer cream cakes and she can cure that. Her hair needs cutting. She needs to slim. She looks a little gormless, perhaps, but I think that is because she is overcome with shyness by the sight of me. It did happen and it made Syb kindly disposed. 'Do go on,' she purred. 'Tell me what is wrong.'

'Ellie, no—' Vida snapped.

Don't be a spoil-sport, Syb said silently.

She went on looking sweetly at Ellie who explained.

'But how exciting,' Syb said. 'London. At your age. Lydia was in Switzerland at eighteen.'

'Lydia,' Vida said, 'did not have a loving home to stay in.'

You cow, Syb thought. But she only laughed and looked at Toby. 'What do you say about Ellie leaving home?'

He was all for it. Syb could believe him.

Ellie said Lydia had promised to stake her until she got a job and could keep herself.

'Lydia will give you nothing,' Vida said. And to Lydia, 'I am not going to stand by and watch you break up my home around my ears. You will give Ellie nothing. She is not going to that dreadful place.'

'Oh, come on, Vida,' Syb said. 'It isn't so bad. Of course it isn't what it was when Toby and I were young—' She let this sink in, then she said she was certain Ellie could manage.

'Perhaps,' Vida told her. 'But I'll thank your daughter, who hasn't enough to do in her own life, to leave Ellie alone and to mind her own business and stop interfering.' She said, 'We were all all right until she came.'

Syb simmered with anger. Ellie said, 'Ma, don't talk like that—'

'You be quiet,' Vida ordered.

Syb looked at them all. Toby was sitting with his eyes shut, aloof from what he probably thought of as the heat of the day. It used to drive me mad, Syb thought, when he did this. 'Open your eyes,' I would shout. 'Look at me.' He wouldn't. He said he wished he could block his ears too.

Vida looked like a simmering volcano. Anyone near her was in danger of being singed.

Lydia looked pale. Syb remembered Lydia hated scenes. Ellie was white so that her poor eye showed up in all its horridness. Poor little newt, Syb thought.

She was going to shoot Vida down once and for all. I'm blowed if I shall sit watching while this awful woman gives my Lydia stick.

She said to Toby, 'You are quite willing that Ellie leave home?'

'I've said so.' He sounded tired at saying it again.

'I am here, you know,' Vida said as

though she had left anyone in doubt. 'It is what I say about Ellie that matters—'

Syb ignored her. 'You type, do you?' she murmured to Ellie. 'Shorthand at some incredible rate?'

Ellie thought she understood, thought she could not possibly be hearing aright, thought it too wonderful, decided to act anyway, and said hoarsely, 'Not at an incredible rate. I am average.' It was said with such patent honesty it was charming. Perhaps Ellie was astute enough to realize that honesty was always the best policy with this woman. Any deceit, any attempt to pull the wool over her eyes, and Syb would throw you out with contemptuous ease, and not take you back.

'Are you offering her a job, Syb?' Toby asked. 'Good show. Who with?'

'With me.'

'No—' Vida almost yelled.

Syb said, 'I need a secretary-companion. Sounds grand but it isn't. Dogsbody, really. Someone to look after things. I find I am growing too old to see to all the detail. Have you ever known, Toby, such an accumulation of paper that follows one around these days?' She wondered who dealt with his paper work, but didn't pause to ask. 'A good home provided,' she told Ellie. 'Can you drive a car? Yes? Well, then—' her tones were dulcet. Circe might have sounded like this.

If so, Vida would have been a great help to Ulysses. 'No,' she said. 'Certainly not.'

'I should very much like to work for you,' Ellie said.

'I don't have a personal maid,' Syb told her. 'They are inclined to think they are indispensable. But I think I can employ a secretary without running the risk of being called spoiled to death.' Her eyes rested on Vida. 'You should suit me, Ellie.'

'Thank you.'

'You will not work for her,' Vida said.

'Ma,' Ellie said quietly, with such venom even Vida was astonished, 'if you try to stop me, I shall go away and never come back.'

'Thirty pounds a week and all found,' Syb said. 'If you satisfy me I shall give you an increase after three months. You won't find it a penny too much. I shall expect you to dress well.'

'When do you want me to start?'

'I am going back to London tomorrow.'

Vida started to say something and Ellie said, 'Ma, shut up—'

'Another thing,' Syb said. 'I shall expect you to sound and act like a lady.'

'She is a lady,' Vida told her.

'It's an old-fashioned word, isn't it?' Syb said.

'I'll pack now,' Ellie said. 'Do you want me to come with you, tonight, wherever you go?'

Syb heard the plea within the words. God help you, newt, she thought, if you stay here.

'Since I am staying with Lydia, you might ask her if there is room for you.'

Ellie asked, Lydia nodded. Ellie thanked her and hurried off. Mentally she was discarding clothes she knew were unsuitable for this new job. It didn't leave much to pack.

Vida rose but Toby told her to sit down. She did. 'Let the girl go, Vida. It's no fun for her here. It's generous of Syb to offer her a job. I hope she does well.' It was quite a speech for Toby.

'Gives satisfaction,' Vida sneered. 'A fine thing. Your daughter at your ex-wife's beck and call.'

'That's a damned sight better than the *milieu* she's found herself in up to now.' It was the first thing Lydia had said for some time. It was like a stone thrown into a pond for they all turned and stared at her.

Vida looked ugly with dislike. She reminded Lydia of a tormented bull in the ring as she swung round to face Lydia. The darts were making their mark from all sides.

But Lydia thought this was the time to tell Ellie's mother a few things Ellie's mother did not know about. She described the party Ellie had taken her to. She told her where Ellie's bruises came from. She said how Ellie had asked for money to go to London. She did not mention the trip to London nor the fifty pounds.

Vida said she was exaggerating if not lying in her teeth.

Syb rose. 'When do we leave?'

'I have to pack too,' Lydia said.

'A nightdress and a toothbrush,' her mother said. 'The rest can be sent. It is only to the top of the hill. Go after Ellie,' she ordered, 'and tell her to do the same. Toothbrush and nightdress. If what she wore tonight is an indication of the state of her wardrobe, better leave it behind.'

'Toby,' Vida said as she would, 'are you

209

going to sit there and let her say these things?'

'Don't be silly,' Toby said, rose and left them. He left them to get on with the final act which he supposed would be a corker. He didn't want to be there when they slanged each other. He bade Syb an amiable goodnight and left.

'When you get tired of her—which you will do because taking her away is only a way of getting at me—she can always come home,' Vida said.

The light will be in the window, Syb thought but did not say it aloud. Contrary to what Toby thought, she did not want any final scene, no more trying to score off Vida. Lydia and Ellie were both out of the room so she said what she thought she should say. 'You and I,' she told Vida, 'are wreckers. We are alike in that.'

'I am not a wrecker. It's what I called your daughter, though, and I am right.'

'You are wrong. Lydia is a builder, not a wrecker. But it's our word, Vida. I because I am too selfish to have given Lydia the home and the love she needed. When you accuse me of that, it's true. And you because you don't want Ellie out of your sight.'

'I want her to have a safe, happy life.'

'You can't guarantee the first. Let her make the other for herself. Toby,' Syb said, 'is Toby. Precious little help from him. He isn't interested. But you and I should know better. I think we have done what we could to make the girls deformed.'

'What a word! You must be mad.'

'Not at the moment. Honest, for once. Lydia is lonely and all too soon puts up a barrier where she is lonelier still.'

'No wonder. You are never around when she wants you.'

'And you are there too much and cram your girl with silliness. She is lonely too.'

'I have never left her for a day if I could help it. We were like sisters until Lydia came worming her way in, mischief-making—'

'Thank heaven it is Lydia,' Syb said. 'It might have been one of Ellie's local friends. I shall take care of her, Vida. Occupied and interested, she may be a different girl.'

'I don't want her different. And what about your girl?' Vida said. 'What happens to her when you dance off with Ellie tomorrow? Do you leave Lydia behind again? I bet,' she said, 'you wish she was married. I bet you eye every young man you meet as a potential son-in-law. So long as he takes her off your hands. Imagine,' Vida said, 'Lydia coming here to try to make a home for herself.'

'Imagine.' But Syb could not argue any more. Most of what Vida was saying was truth and Syb felt tears close. Wreckers, both of them.

'Goodbye, Ma,' Ellie said, taking her courage in both hands and coming to say goodbye in the sitting-room. Vida only turned a suffering cheek and said, 'Don't say I didn't warn you.'

Nobody asked against what. Ellie fled.

When they reached the house at the top of the hill, Ellie asked Lydia if she might have a few minutes here in the car with Syb as she had something to say. Lydia guessed what it was and left them together.

'There is something I must tell you,' Ellie said. 'When you've heard what it is, if you change your mind—'

'You know you would rather die than let that happen. Out with it.'

'I took fifty pounds of Lydia's money and went to London. I told myself I would pay it back, and I meant to. But heaven knows when I should be able to.' There it was said, and Ellie sat staring out of the window of the car, her face turned from Syb. She heard Syb say, 'You pinch anything of mine and I'll have the police on you. Come on. Let's go in!'

Ellie could have died for this woman.

And Syb believed she had a bargain in Ellie. Fortuitous, Syb thought, me turning up when she wanted someone. It will be fun to see how the child makes out. I think she can be presentable when she smartens herself up and thins down.

Poor little devil.

Syb was right. She did get a bargain in Ellie, who worked hard and loyally for this woman she adored. Ellie forgot her home with indecent haste.

Cherry was delighted with visitors. 'I am no visitor,' Lydia said. 'I am here for good now.' Cherry said 'Hurrah—'

'The place looks a picture,' Syb said when she and Lydia were on their own at last. 'Polished with loving care. Though it has an empty feeling. Tell me the history of that pretty little Jenny Wren.'

So Lydia told her Cherry's story which was Duke's story too. 'Of course she will marry him,' Syb said. 'You know where happy marriages are made. I am certain theirs is recorded Up There, at this moment.'

Lydia nodded while silently praying, 'Don't enquire. Don't ask. Because I shall have to say no, there is no one, no Duke Beverley in my life, the name making my heart beat faster, as I am sure Cherry's heart beats faster. No one, do you hear?'

'What are you thinking of?' she heard Syb say.

'The Ark.' Syb, as well she might, looked surprised. Lydia said, 'They are pairing off. Cherry and Duke. Now you and Ellie have met and struck a spark.'

'The sparks are Vida's—'

'Even Vida has Toby.' Lydia stopped speaking. A minute ago she had prayed Syb would not mention a man and marriage. Now, she had played into Syb's hands. Sometimes you couldn't get away from it. Men and marriage. But Syb was kind. She thought Lydia looked tired to the bone so no prying tonight.

'I am taking a flat in Regents Park. Visit me there.'

Lydia promised that she would. 'How long will you stay?'

'It depends.' Syb did not say on what. It depended if she found something in her unremitting search, something she might offer Connie Coles.

Next morning, Ellie said to Syb at breakfast, 'Do you think I should follow you to London on another train?'

'Don't you want to be seen with me?'

'I have to do some shopping,' Ellie confessed. 'I have nothing smart enough.' She looked and sounded twelve years of age. Gone all the silly brazenness.

'Is there a place in Wadden where I might help you shop?' Syb asked.

She is being kind, Lydia thought. It augured well for Ellie's future. Ellie said there was such a place. 'I've never bought anything there. Lydia has. But then, it's the sort of place Lydia would shop at—'

'We are not discussing Lydia,' Syb said.

'No. Well, it's the place for—for country clothes. You know? Tweeds and cashmere. It's expensive but the clothes are lovely—'

'You can pay me back,' Syb said. When Cherry came in with fresh coffee, she was off on another tack. 'Cherry, get particulars of that school, at once, and send them down to me. If it's suitable, Will must

215

go there.' She explained to Lydia. 'Cherry tells me there is a good school here. Will is a bright boy. I shall send him there if we—Cherry and I—think it is suitable.'

'You are enjoying yourself,' Lydia said.

'Should I have had six children?' Syb wondered.

12

Perhaps it was as well for Lydia, pitch-forked so to speak into her new home, that she had a visitor almost immediately. A week later Alec arrived for the holiday she had mentioned to him and which he was looking forward to. It wasn't that Lydia was depressed, exactly, at having to remove herself from Vida's presence. Rather that she had gone there, to Vida and Toby, with such high hopes of becoming one of the family, and all she had done, she told herself, was to make a king-size enemy of Vida. And if Amalie ever knew of the deceit Duke and Lydia practised on her in London, Vida would have a stout ally. The Kettle Sisters Ride Again!

Amalie had not been to Vida's since that time. So Cherry had seen nothing of Duke. He telephoned her, though, and one day Lydia came upon her standing staring at the telephone after Duke had rung off. Easy to see in Cherry's face what she was thinking.

Lydia put her arm round her shoulders and hugged her. 'I have no crystal ball but I must say that I cannot, at my most despairing, see Amalie married to him. Something will happen to stop it. It must, and when it does, grab him.'

'I shall.'

The next day Syb arrived for a flying visit to take Cherry and Will with her to the school she had decided would do for him. Will sat the examination that day and passed with flying colours. 'We never had any doubts,' Syb said. 'Buy his school uniform and send the bill to me,' she told Cherry. 'He will look like they all look, swamped by it.' 'I'll take a snapshot of him wearing it,' Cherry said, 'and send you a copy.' Syb, after a moment's thought, found she liked this. Was she, she wondered, growing sentimental in middle age? Maybe. She told Lydia that what she liked about young Mrs Matthews was that she wasted no time telling her oh, she shouldn't do such-and-such, it was too good of her. 'False, that sort of thing,' Syb said. 'She thanked me for giving Will his chance and said she would do everything she could to see he made the most of it. That boy,' Syb said, 'could be

Prime Minister one day. Though why wish the fate on him?'

Will was taken with Syb. Here was someone like himself who knew what two and two made, who knew black from white. Will liked such clear cut thinking. Mrs Farmer could smile and be pleasant but you do something she disapproved of and bingo! you copped it. Will wasn't going to cop it, not if he could help it. He was going to show her she had backed a winner.

Lucy continued to enchant all who came in touch with her. Even Ben Bartlow, who didn't much care for children, liked Lucy. He and Lucy and Will had met. Will and he had long talks about London. And about other things. 'A nice pair of children,' he told Vida.

'Common as dirt,' she said. 'you can see. I don't know where Lydia met her but she is being taken in by her. I wouldn't have her as my hairdresser.'

She was right there. Cherry would never come.

The first half of Alec's holiday was delightful. They drove to the coast and took Lucy with them. Lucy had reservations about the sea. It was too big. But she adored rock pools. And they adored her in her bathing suit with her bucket and spade. 'Do you remember being that age?' Lydia asked him. He shook his head. She said that it was when she passed babies on outings in their prams that she felt the greatest unfairness. 'At the sitting up against cushions stage. There I am, shoving my way through the crowd, loaded with parcels like a yak, and there they are, the pedestrians parting like the waters of the Red Sea to let them through! Boy babies put me in mind of Edward the Seventh, lolling there, particularly portly ones. Miniature monarchs, every last one of them, pushed everywhere by adults, not having to make an effort to do anything. I envy them and I can't remember what it was like.' Her aggrieved tone made him laugh. When she was like this he thought her delightful.

He thought he was in love with her.

So the days passed happily, and Cherry got almost as much happiness from seeing Lydia happy as when she herself was with Duke. He and Amalie had arrived yesterday. He hadn't paid Cherry a visit yet but she knew she would not have to wait long. They might not have long in each other's company but it would be long enough for her to find out at first hand how he was, what he had done since she had seen him last, to ask if he had written any stories. His replies she would store in her mind to mull over and remember when he had left.

But until the day when perhaps Duke would leave Amalie (or Amalie order him out, Cherry didn't mind) Cherry thought she must do all she could for Lydia and Alec Bartlow. She was certain he was in love with Lydia. With Lydia there was no telling. That cool face gave little away if Lydia did not wish it to.

Then the happy time exploded and disintegrated in a fury of anger and spite no one could have anticipated.

It was Ben who lit the fuse.

On Amalie's first day with Vida, she told Vida at breakfast she and Duke would not be there until evening. They were going to visit friends. 'A nice thing,' Vida said. 'You come here to me and then someone else is more important.' Amalie took no notice. She never did. Vida's maunderings, she called them.

So Vida and Ben, that afternoon, sat in

the sitting-room. 'Toby playing golf,' Vida said. 'Amalie gone visiting. Ellie lost to me. I only have you, Ben. My Old Faithful.' She gave him a smile, asking herself as she so often did what on earth he would do if it weren't for her. She didn't say it aloud because even she might have been bored hearing it by now.

Ben sympathized with her these days. Personally, he thought Ellie fortunate to get away to London where she could see different things, meet people and get out of this rural rut. Ben himself had loved London. But he kept silent now while Vida went back over Ellie's life, to little girl days, school days, up to the present.

And Ben really listened, not pretended to listen. This was one of the good things about him. It was what made it easy for people to confide in him.

But, as he had told Alec, Vida wasn't interested in what he knew about the old days so he let her do the talking. Sometimes, he tossed her a morsel of gossip. If it did not interest her, she ignored it. But sometimes, like a seal, she caught it.

There was a bowl of roses on the table between them and Ben thought the scent

222

was exquisite. He took a rose and held it between his fingers. 'Put it back,' Vida said. 'You will spoil my arrangement. I'm glad you aren't an old man who wears a rose in his buttonhole. They irritate me.'

Early June, Ben was thinking. June, the month of roses. June brides. He remembered weddings he had been to. From the Abbey itself to weddings in the country. Pretty brides, handsome brides, shy or brazen, tall or short. He wondered where they were and what had happened to them. He had always liked a June wedding. The scent of roses, and a bride with a wreath of white roses, and bridesmaids with bouquets ...

'What are you smiling at?' Vida said but didn't wait for an answer. 'Amalie is besotted with Lydia Farmer,' she grumbled. 'She said she was really disappointed Lydia isn't here and how could I let her go? One thing about Amalie I disapprove of. Money and position are apt to blind her to people's faults. That man she works for. She makes him sound as if he had just come down from the mountain with the tablets under his arm! I don't suppose Lydia knew him as well as she made out. Still, Amalie trusts her—'

'She has no cause to,' Ben said.

Vida looked at him. 'What do you mean?' She put down her knitting and stared at him.

So Ben told Vida what Will had told him about the time Will's mother was ill and Lydia and Duke looked after the family.

Ben Bartlow and Will Matthews met from time to time when Will flew his kite on the common. There were seats on the common and Will joined Ben once or twice while his mother and Lucy shopped. Ben's sympathetic attitude had worked on Will too. Will talked. He told him about the time Miss Farmer looked after them. He believed she had given the slip to the person she was staying with, Will thought in the flat where his mother had cooked the Christmas goose. 'Then she pretended to go home but she didn't. She came to us, and she took us to Brighton. She's smashing. Miss Farmer.'

Ben did not repeat this bit.

'You mean she deceived Amalie?' Vida said. 'And that man too? What a pair. I always knew he was no good. She bought Amalie a dress and took her to the Savoy. If I had heard that once—' Vida shook her head. 'Conscience money! The sly puss.'

She was silent for a few seconds, then said, more strongly, 'The liar! You know, Ben, I have never trusted her. I said before she came she would bring trouble. She looks as if butter won't melt in her mouth. She acts as if she is a cut above the rest of us. Then she treats Amalie like that, making a fool of her, with that creature as accomplice. I've said Amalie should send him packing. What Lydia wants—I can see it—is to ruin Amalie's life too. She wants him to marry that Matthews woman. I hope he does. Amalie is too good for him.' She did not say, she did not have to, 'Wait until I tell her this.' What she did say, fatefully, was 'How did Alec know Lydia was staying here? Something about Syb meeting him in New York—'

Ben nodded.

'Did she ask him to come looking for Lydia?' Vida said. She had a feeling that she was on the eve of what she could only describe to herself as something big.

A feeling that things were snowballing.

And she listened without interruption when Ben, at the moment, went off at a tangent. He did this sometimes, talked about what had happened in the past instead of staying with the present, and usually it annoyed Vida who dragged him sharply back to the current time and place. But today she let him talk. She might pick up a clue, she thought.

'What I heard,' he said, 'reminded me of my sister when she Came Out. Her Season,' he explained kindly to Vida, who nodded, only just not telling him she knew what a Season was, a Summer junketing for girls whose parents had too much money, a marriage mart. But this was what Ben was coming to. 'My sister was a plain girl, a flop, you might say. Two Seasons and not a nibble. So my mother got hold of this young man. I don't know if she paid him. I do know she got him to pay court to my sister, to take an interest in her. It worked. My sister bloomed like a rose. And ran away with a groom.'

'You mean,' breathed Vida, 'that Lydia's mother ordered Alec Bartlow to come here and pretend to take an interest in the girl so that it might—do her good?' She sounded as if she could hardly believe it.

'That's right. Pretend he found her fascinating. Alec and I were talking about Syb. I said I didn't think she considered Lydia all that much, and he said I was wrong. He said she had asked him to come here and give Lydia a whirl. You mentioned Lydia's conscience. Probably it soothed Syb's conscience, when she has such a good time herself, to do something for her daughter.'

Ben really was a gossip. Now that he had Vida's attention he was making the most of it.

To give Vida her due, she told herself she didn't think much of a man who repeated such things. What Ben did not tell her was that Alec had gone on to say, 'At first I thought it a joke. Then, when I saw that she was serious, I thought Syb was having a rush of mother love to the head. She meant well.' He had said that, meeting Lydia, he didn't have to pretend. He thought her a charming girl. Not a cracker like Syb. But charming.

Ben did not say any of this because it wasn't what Vida wanted to hear. They were having such a pleasant afternoon, why spoil it?

Vida put aside her knitting, and rose. 'What would you like for tea? Pancakes? You love pancakes. I'll make pancakes for you. It will be a bit of trouble but that's all right. You just sit at the kitchen table and eat them hot from the pan. The only way to eat them.'

Ben was greedy. The thought of Vida's pancakes, with sugar and lemon, made his mouth water.

Thirty pieces of silver.

Pancakes straight from the pan.

Amalie arrived home too late to talk to Vida that evening. It will keep, Vida told herself. Next day, she took Amalie with her to her own room, telling her she had something to say which she thought Amalie should hear. She closed the door and said, forthrightly, 'Where is Duke?'

'Gone for a walk.'

'Gone up the hill, no doubt.'

But Amalie was standing at the window, looking down at the garden. In her mind's eye she might have seen another garden and another view for when she spoke she said, with a degree of wistfulnes, 'Enid is home again. I shouldn't be surprised if she asks Lydia there. They don't entertain much but Lydia is bound to be asked. I should like to see their home, I must admit.'

'Don't be a fool. Turn round and listen to me.'

Amalie turned and frowned. But the retort she was going to give on the unwarranted rudeness died on her lips when Vida started to speak, and Vida spoke succinctly, wasting no time, coming to the point. She repeated what Ben had told her about the time when Cherry Matthews was ill and needed help, when Duke and Lydia, as Vida said, pulled the wool over Amalie's eyes. 'She made a right fool of you. I told Ben—'

'I don't want you discussing me with that old fool.'

'Just as well I did or you wouldn't know what you should know. She mesmerized you, that girl. Because she met your boss once, or said that she did. She is poison, Amalie. She found a way for Duke and that woman to meet behind your back, while she was your guest. I've seen the Matthews woman. She is common as dirt.' Vida was enjoying herself. 'Amalie, you can do better than think of marrying that awful man.'

Did Amalie, when she was honest with herself, know that this was not so? She had never been able to keep a man for long because she always wanted to change their natures into some image she herself preferred, and they would not stand for it and left her. She admitted she was sometimes what she called hard on Duke but only for his own good. He wasted his life. If he only listened to her, surely it wasn't too late, even now, to make a success of it.

Did she think he was malleable where the others had told her to mind her own business? Perhaps. But even she must have known he was kinder than most people. She did know that when they were married he would never leave her. Anyway, who would want to take Duke from her? Funny-looking, scarecrow-looking Duke.

He was her insurance against a lonely old age.

'He is smitten with the woman,' she heard Vida say. 'Taking her to your flat at Christmas. The cheek! Lying to you, telling you he has been to the pub when he was probably with her. He and Lydia staying with her in some slummy little hole. Amalie, are you going to take all this lying down?'

Amalie said nothing. Vida thought her a cold fish. If it were she who was getting this eye-opener, she would be in hysterics by now. She said, 'And that isn't all I heard.'

'You had a field day.'

'I haven't noticed you've told me to stop! Amalie, Ben told me that Alec told him Lydia's mother practically begged Alec to come here and pretend to be smitten by Lydia to see if it would put some sparkle in her.'

'Don't be ridiculous. That doesn't happen these days.'

'That's what I thought but Ben says Alec told him about it. Amalie, aren't men awful? Imagine telling! Of course,' Vida said, 'he may have plans of his own. All that money. I don't suppose some men would mind a dull rich wife.'

'Duke is back.' Amalie, without another word to her sister, left the room and went downstairs. From the window Vida watched them go out through the gate and start up the hill together. 'That will fix Lydia, once and for all,' Vida said aloud.

Amalie told Duke she had to see Lydia. A whole day had gone by and she had not called on her good friend. She put her arm through his and they walked up together. Duke didn't mind. It was a chance to see Cherry.

Alec Bartlow was in Wadden so Lydia took the brunt of what came.

She welcomed them in. Amalie shut the sitting-room door behind them, then sat opposite Lydia and began her tirade. She told her she knew the truth of what had taken place when Lydia stayed with her, earlier in the year. One glance at Duke and Lydia knew this was the first time he knew Amalie was cognisant of what had happened. Almost helplessly they smiled at each other, which smile only fanned Amalie's fury.

'Amusing,' she agreed. 'Deceiving me like that. When you were my guest—'

'It was unforgivable,' Lydia said. 'I take the blame. I thought it up—'

'No one planned anything,' Duke said. 'It just happened. One thing followed on another—'

'Oh, I don't suppose you needed much help,' Amalie told him. 'You managed quite well on your own at Christmas, inviting that slut into my home.'

For the moment, they did not know whom she meant. Lydia said, 'Use that word again and I shall ask you to leave. I should make you apologize to Mrs Matthews only I don't want her dragged into this brawl. She is a friend of mine.'

'I am sure she is. I hope you treat her better than some people who thought they were your friends,' Amalie said. 'You with your showing-off, name dropping, throwing your money around, thinking a meal at a posh hotel would make up for your deceit.'

'You do bring out the worst in me,' Lydia said. She supposed Duke would stay and see the whole sorry thing through. She wished he was not there. One thing, from this day on, Duke and Amalie were through with each other. From this day on, Cherry had hope. It was worth putting up with what was going on, though Lydia hated scenes. They made her feel sick.

'You think money buys everything,' she heard Amalie accuse her. 'You dangled it in front of Ellie until her brain was addled. You've bought this Matthews woman though I don't suppose, with that sort, it was difficult.'

Duke made to interrupt. She took no notice. 'And I suppose you think it will buy you a man.'

'Get out,' Lydia said, adding, absurdly, 'please.'

'For I have heard another piece of news—' Amalie said.

'Gossip,' Duke translated.

'If you like. I heard that Alec Bartlow was told by your mother to come and see you. Oh, not in the ordinary way. Not "When you are in those parts, call on my daughter, see how she is getting on". Oh no,' said Amalie. 'Your mother begged him to come here and take you around a bit. "Pretend to take an interest", your mother said. "No one does". And if you want to know how I know—and I can see by your face you don't disbelieve me—Alec Bartlow told Ben, and that garrulous old fool told Vida.'

'Amalie—' Duke said, and his voice was terrible in its anger, Amalie didn't even look at him. 'What a thing to have to do,' she said, in mock astonishment. 'Practically to beg someone to pretend an interest! I'll say this for your mother, I don't suppose it happened to her. But then, I expect she is wondering what the

234

hell to do about you. At her wits' end, when she remembers. Twenty-five and unmarried. These days when girls marry at sixteen.'

They could, if they had cared, mention that Amalie was still unwed and older than Lydia.

'I don't believe a word of it,' Duke said. He looked at Lydia and he knew she believed it. He thought it must have happened before and he said nothing more. There was nothing one could say.

Amalie said, 'Ben and Vida were chuckling about it when I went in to them. I asked them what the joke was and Vida told me. She said that at least she had never come to that, never had to try to persuade one of the local lads to take Ellie around. On the contrary.'

'Have you finished?' Lydia said. 'I did ask you to go. And I don't think I have to tell you you will not be welcome here again.'

'I don't want to come. I don't want to see either of you,' Amalie said. 'Good luck to you. You all three deserve each other.' Then she left.

Duke let her go, then left himself.

When Cherry came into the room, she

said, 'There was a row. I heard her—'

'I'll tell you what she said,' Lydia said, and did. Then, 'If he asks you to marry him, say yes. I told you to grab him. Do it. You can be married from this house. I don't know when he will be back. He may take a bit of time to get over things. It wasn't pretty.'

'What about you?'

'I'm going out.'

'What shall I tell Alec?'

For once, Lydia, that girl with the very good manners, only shrugged.

When she returned, late in the evening, Alec was waiting for her. 'Next time you drive off, walk off, even swim off, leave me a note. All I know is what Cherry could tell me.'

But she told herself she was the old cool Lydia now. The anger was gone. Anger with Amalie, anger with Syb, with this man for gossiping. People are as they are. You'll not change them. So just take what comes.

A philosopher, yet? Perhaps. She thought she had need to be.

She wasn't in love with Alec Bartlow. Nowhere near love. He had been a pleasant companion, she had enjoyed his company. This was all.

'Where did you go?' He took her by the shoulders and made her face him. She laughed, and he reddened and dropped his hands.

'I took a drive.'

'Have you eaten?' It sounded sweet and solicitous, it almost got under her defences, this homely question.

'Yes,' she lied. 'I am going away tomorrow.'

'Where?'

'To Paris. I need some clothes.'

(Ben and Vida were laughing about it.) How could he, this man she had liked and thought her friend, have told Ben? It was out of character. Or was it?

'That's a good line,' he said, trying to make her smile. She didn't. He said, 'Lydia, what have I done?'

'Oh, for Pete's sake,' she said, impatiently, and the silly little phrase seemed somehow to give more truth to her words than studied diction. 'That silly question. *What have I done?* It's maddening. In school, when one was bored with someone, and it happens, when you just wanted them to go away, you could bet it would come out. *What have I done?* As if they were important enough—'

237

'All right,' he said. 'All right. I get it. You want to be on your own. You have a sudden whim to go to Paris. Why don't you say so without all this build up? I'll go back to London. You go to Paris. Let's do it amicably.' Then he said, 'I want to ask you something.'

'What?'

'Marry me.'

She laughed. It was the laugh that did it. Without a word he left.

13

A mental abberation, Lydia thought. Alec Bartlow proposing to me. It slipped out. Guilt, probably. He couldn't have meant it so you forget it. Anyway, there was no need now to go to Paris. Alec had left early before she herself was up.

Cherry, while upset at what had happened to Lydia, was only human. The man who filled her thoughts was not Alec. Lydia understood.

'Where do you think Duke is?' Cherry asked.

'Not far away. Probably in the village. I think he knows the man who owns the pub by the river.'

'He goes a lot to pubs.'

'So would we if we had lived with Amalie. He will spend more time at home now. Cherry, take the shopping list and go down to the village and look for him.'

'Lydia?' Cherry said imploringly.

'All right. Give me the shopping list.'

Lydia and Duke met on the bridge that

239

spanned the little river the other side of the village, not the broad river that flowed down to the sea a few miles away. This was what Will called a baby river. Bright and clear over rounded stones and sand so clean it looked scrubbed. But to Lydia the best sight at this moment was Duke's lanky figure bent over the parapet, apparently engrossed in what he could see below. 'A fish,' he said. 'Takes me back to when I was a boy. We used to look over the bridge and try to spot the fish. I never have been a fisherman,' he admitted. 'I just can't bring myself to use that damned hook. Soft, that's me.'

Lydia did not say whether she shared his qualms or not but stood beside him. Then they both pointed at the same time to the small slim shape below. Turning, they beamed at one another. 'I almost cried *Eureka,*' she said. 'Come to lunch.'

'I must talk to you first. You are her best friend.'

So they left the village and walked slowly along the country road which made so delightful a change from the car-ridden main road. Hedges were thick here, starred with wild roses. There was for good measure a stile to a field. They leaned against it. 'All I want is a straw in my mouth,' Duke said. 'I have the makings of a yokel.'

'You will soon be a married man with two step-children.'

'I want to marry her.'

'Of course. She loves you. You must marry her. She is waiting for you to ask. I told her that she must grab you, when you do ask.'

'You said that?'

'I know a good man when I see one—'

He laughed. 'Bless you. Will I be good for the children, do you think?'

'Yes,' she said without hesitation. 'A wonderful father. Will is going to feel relieved when the burden of man about the house falls from his shoulders like Pilgrim's pack. He has done well but he's a small boy, after all. And imagine being Lucy's step-father! Imagine watching Lucy grow up beautifully and happily. You are fortunate. Oh, Cherry and the children and your children and Cherry's will be happy. Don't you worry.'

'I shall find a job here.'

'Will you mind leaving London?'

He said with feeling, 'Hell, no.'

'There is a good bookshop in Wadden,'

Lydia said. 'I am certain you will find a job there. When I was there recently they were short-staffed. And I'm going to sound as bossy as my mother when I say you should stay at the house. Don't look a gift horse in the mouth,' she told him. 'Stay there with Cherry. Will is happy. I need Cherry—'

He thought what a fount of kindness she had. Here she was working overtime to sell him the idea they would do her a favour by staying on. He said, 'Thank you. But when you marry—'

'You move out? I've no plans to marry.' Now she looked severe again. He thought with amusement how the clouds closed in over her face as over a sunny sky. One moment she was laughing, a pretty young woman. The next, her face was shadowed. She looked as she had looked when he first met her. Alone to the point of being lonely. Here was someone, he thought, who needed friends more than most people, always to be in the company of someone she liked and who liked her, a girl who slipped only too quickly behind a self-imposed barrier.

He told her plans had nothing to do with it. You sweep a man off his feet and wham! He said, 'I can imagine you doing that, sweeping a man off his feet.' He meant it. But she said candidly, 'I can't imagine it. A person as prosaic as I am—'

'You are a raving romantic! Like me.'

'Yes, well,' she said. 'Let's get back to you. Stay at the house. Look after it for me. Look on it as your home. I don't suppose I shall be there all that much.'

'Where are you going?' He looked so disappointed she warmed towards him.

'On my travels, I suppose. There isn't much for me here.'

'I thought you were home for good now.'

The trouble is, she thought, I don't know where home is. Lydia Farmer, that enviable person, with two houses to her name and not one home.

Home is where the heart is.

She wondered where Alec was?

In London, you fool. He hasn't had time to make arrangements to get to Africa to shoot big game. Besides, he has a job.

Over lunch, they discussed the wedding, discussed it sensibly, planned sensibly, though two out of three present sat with smiles on their faces which never seemed to slip, Lydia thought. When they discussed the wedding, they smiled. They embraced

243

Lydia into their joy and she was grateful and tried hard not to spoil things for them.

'Have you left much at the flat?' she heard Cherry ask. Lydia thought that whatever he had left he might find thrown into a black plastic bag for the dustmen to collect if Amalie had her way!

'Will you go there to collect it? Oh, Duke, no.' Cherry was suddenly fearful that if he did go she might not see him again. He said he would go up tomorrow and arrange for a Special Licence. And when he said this, Cherry forgot completely that wicked witch, Amalie Kettle, as Duke meant her to. Cherry was transported into a world with Duke where there were no witches nor warlocks, no Amalie, because Duke would not let it happen. Lydia thought he was one of the kindest men she had ever known.

When they were on their own, Cherry told her husband-to-be, with the loving-all-the-world feeling that comes over a woman herself in love, that she wished Lydia could be certain of a happy ending. 'I wish we could help them.'

'There are people,' he said, 'who don't much care for others to toil on their behalf.

Capable people. Lydia and Bartlow both seem capable.'

'Practical,' Cherry said. 'But they are often the stubbornnest and most stupid about managing their own affairs. I think we should try to help.' She looked so comical, furrowing her brow and biting her lip in concentration, he laughed and kissed her.

'That poisonous bit about her mother sending him here to—to see what he could do with Lydia,' Cherry said, hardly able to bring the words out. 'It's ridiculous. If it were someone else, Lydia would tell her to laugh at it. But I know her by now. She is really hurt. And it's because she likes Alec, probably loves him. So she is sensitive about his good opinion.'

'Lucy will know where to turn when she needs things explained,' Duke said admiringly. 'Lucky Lucy.'

'Never mind Lucy for the moment,' said Lucy's loving mother. 'Lydia is so sensible, so intelligent about everything else. But then, not many women are intelligent in love.'

'Aren't they?'

'If I had been sensible,' she said, 'I might not have clung to the thought that things

245

would come right for you and me. I wish we could find Lydia a goose.'

That evening, making certain Lydia did not overhear, Cherry telephoned London. 'May I speak plainly?' she asked Syb. And did.

So Duke Beverley went out of Amalie's flat and out of her life. (He did get the job in the bookshop at Wadden. They were glad to have him.) Amalie made a tale out of it to anyone who would listen, and no one, if they could help it, listened twice. Cherry she disguised as a *femme fatale*. A temptress it had been impossible to thwart. Amalie went on working hard and loyally for J.G. and one afternoon met Mrs J.G., the gentle Enid, when she called at the office. Amalie mentioned Lydia, perhaps hoping Mrs J.G. would say she had never heard of her. On the contrary. Mrs J.G. enthused over Lydia. 'She is over here, you say? I should like to get in touch. Do you know where she is?' Pretending regret, Amalie said she was sorry, she did not.

When Alec Bartlow received Syb Farmer's invitation to dine with her, his first instinct was to refuse. But he went, Syb was someone you did not easily say no to.

He would not believe that Lydia had confided in her about his proposal of marriage. In his own words, he was damn certain the girl would pretend it had never happened.

Syb had sent Ellie to the cinema so that they had the flat to themselves. 'The child is slimming,' Syb said. 'So it is kinder to send her out than to let her see what we eat.' Then she told Alec what had happened. 'Poor darling,' she said of Lydia. 'And of course we can't bring the subject up, it is far too sensitive a thing, unless she tells us about it. That nice Cherry Matthews told me. I really do approve of people who come out with the truth,' Syb told him. 'If it is called going behind someone's back, well there it is. But it does help to possess the facts.' She was silent, thinking it over, then sighed. 'I can't expect Lydia to believe I did it for her sake. I liked you and I thought it would be fun for her. But it was a lazy thing to do. I should have gone over to her oftener, wherever she was, and made certain she was happy. Now it has been blown up out of all proportion.'

And to give Syb her due she never once,

then or at any time, confronted Alec with his own part in the affair. He was ashamed and sorry. He had told Ben but gone on to say that once he had seen Lydia he had not wanted to go on seeing her for her own sake. Then Ben saw fit to tell Vida. Vida told Amalie. And Amalie made the circle complete.

He was appalled. He believed he knew how sensitive Lydia was. Small wonder she had refused him when he mentioned marriage. And what a time he had chosen! The Fairy Carabosse herself must have had a hand in it. Lost in his thoughts, he did not hear what Syb said. She repeated it. 'I said you are in love with her.'

'I asked her to marry me.'

'And?'

'She laughed.'

Syb tut-tutted. 'It is what I want more than anything—'

'You do? Tell me,' he said, 'did you have it in mind from the time we met? That I fall in love with her and ask her to marry me?'

'What mother wouldn't? You and she are perfect for one another. But she said no.'

'She laughed.'

Syb hid her own smile. How vain men are. She said, 'And you are giving up on the strength of one chuckle?'

He only knew that laugh seared his mind.

'If she is laughing at anything it is at the pernicious timing of all this,' Syb said. 'You must try again.'

She sounded bossy and he rebelled against it. Masculine dignity surfaced. He said, 'I am a busy man. I travel a lot. I haven't all that time to chase a young woman with an eye to matrimony.'

Pompousness was creeping in.

'Of course not,' Syb soothed. 'A busy man and a sensible man. I am certain you lose no sleep over it.'

Also an honest man. He struggled momentarily with the truth but had to admit it. 'I sleep as well as I did.'

'Good,' Syb said cordially. 'We can't have it interfering with your work.'

Suspiciously he looked at her. Blandly she looked back. He said, 'But there are signs and portents that I'm not what I used to be. I used to think I might buy a little cottage where the fishing is good. Or buy a small place in Pembroke, a county I have given my heart to—'

'And now—?'

'The thought of going somewhere on my own just doesn't appeal. I am not self-sufficient any more.'

What an admission. What an honest man, she thought, as well as a charmer. We must indeed have him in the family. There was still hope, she was certain of it.

She said, 'I'll invite Lydia here, this weekend. Come to lunch on Sunday. She loves elephants.'

He said, when he could, 'Flowers I can manage. Elephants I might find difficult.'

'The Zoo,' Syb said, nodding in its direction. 'Take her there on Sunday afternoon. Seeing the elephants may mellow her.'

'Let us be frank,' he said. 'She will see me, know it's a put-up job—don't you think she may tell herself you have connived enough?' It was frank to the point of brutality.

'I shall just keep on trying,' Syb said.

Next day she telephoned Lydia to say she was feeling off colour. Nothing serious. Lydia was not to worry but after all Syb said, we are none of us getting any younger. No, she did not think she need see a doctor. Not at the moment, anyway. No, Lydia was not to come to town. No need.

Lydia arrived at the flat on Friday to find Syb restored to health and good spirits and delighted to see her. They spent Saturday shopping. Syb said she didn't know what had been wrong, earlier in the week, but she was fine now. Connie Coles was coming over, next week. She and Connie might take a holiday together.

'Connie won't help you take things easy.'

'She will make me laugh. You will stay over the weekend?'

Lydia said she would.

When Alec arrived on Sunday she told herself she should have known it would happen. Syb's machinations. Syb said vigorously she hadn't known he was coming. He lied with as much vigour. 'You brought flowers on the off chance—' Lydia said.

'Yes.'

'What do you do with them when the person they are meant for isn't in?'

'I take them home again. I have a thrifty nature, being an accountant.'

After lunch he told them he planned to

spend the afternoon at the Zoo. It was something he had promised himself for some time. He asked Syb if she would like to go with him. She said regretfully she didn't really feel up to it. She hadn't been too well, lately, which was why Lydia was here. But Lydia might like to go. 'If you feel off colour,' Lydia said, 'shouldn't I stay with you?'

No need for this, Syb told her. So Alec and Lydia left.

'Do you think she will marry him?' Ellie said. 'Ma used to say he might be after her money.'

'I can hear Ma say it. But money need not come between a man and a woman. On the contrary. I should think the absence of it would cause a deep rift, easily.'

'Then I had better try to save,' Ellie said. 'Because I shan't inherit much.'

'Neither are you to think of wedlock for some time,' Syb commanded. 'I have no intention of letting you go. You are too useful.' It might, to an outsider, sound selfish. It was bells ringing for Ellie.

The first creatures Lydia wanted to see were, of course, the elephants.

'It is true,' she said. 'They are my

favourites above everything. Huge, wrinkled, patient, placid. Here, at any rate, they are placid. Do you know,' she said though he hadn't argued with her, *elephants are beautiful.*'

She said it so loudly that a man beside her, complete with string of children, said, 'That's right, lady. Elephants is beautiful.' He chuckled. So did the children, all save the baby, who, stretched on a push chair, slept. 'You see,' Lydia told Alec. 'That is what I mean. To be pushed around, this hot day. To stretch a fat leg or open one eye, then shut it again. To doze. To be treated like a king. And later, when you are grown up, not to be able to remember how it felt!'

'I have never known a woman besotted with elephants,' Alec said. 'Certainly I have never loved one as I do you. Lydia, marry me.'

Now, they were near the sea lion pool. 'Draped on that rock,' she said, 'they look like slugs.' But she did not answer what he had said and he wasn't going to repeat it. Not here.

'Do you want to see the tiger? Or will you shed tears because the beautiful thing is caged?'

253

'Very likely. I should like to see the sea horses.'

She was enchanted with them. 'Up and down—' he heard her murmur to herself. 'Like a waltz on a carousel.'

'Those sea lions,' he said. 'Not slugs. More like jelly babies to me. Come to the Reptile House.' Perhaps she was afraid of snakes, a lot of women are, and would clutch at his arm while she took terrified peeps. She pronounced the snakes gorgeous and gravely studied them.

Once outside, 'Where now?' he asked.

She wanted to renew acquaintance with marmots. 'Look, standing with their paws clasped as though they are praying.'

'I am praying,' he said.

'You are?' She looked surprised.

'Yes.' He said, 'Praying for an answer to what I asked.'

She turned towards him. 'It's a corny old plot, don't you think?'

'The marmots?'

'Not the marmots. No one would write it today. A plot like that. Dowdy girl. Man takes an interest. And whoops! The glamour was there all the time only she hadn't known how to turn the tap on.'

'It wasn't like that at all—'

254

'All right. Not for you. It is Syb who is corny.'

He could not reply to this. He only said, again, 'Will you, Lydia? Marry me?'

'No. Thank you. Have you seen enough?'

'Yes.'

'I thought you had. Well, I haven't,' she said. And, with a charming smile, told him that if he didn't mind she would like to see the rest on her own. 'Nothing diminishes one's pleasure in a place or a visit to something as the company of a second person glowering at one's elbow. I don't often come to the Zoo. I don't want it spoiled.'

'I'm sorry I spoiled it for you,' he said stiffly.

'Well, now you know—' Her smile was kind as she turned it upon him.

'How will you get back?'

'On my own two feet. I shall walk across the Park. Have you noticed,' she said, 'how pastoral the Park can seem after a few hours spent here, watching the animals? With imagination enough, one is transported to Africa, India, anywhere. Then, when one leaves, there are trees and grass and roses. A sweet shock,' she said.

'No,' he said politely, 'I hadn't noticed.

I suppose I will, next time I come.'

'Do you come often?'

'Yes,' he said. But he didn't offer to take her again. They said goodbye, pleasantly, in a civilized fashion. He left and she went to look at the giraffes.

14

Syb did not take disappointment easily. When Lydia returned alone, she rounded on her. 'Here I've sat, dreaming of you and that pleasant young man married, starting a family. I have told myself you would probably have a house in London but a cottage in the country. You would sell the house you are in now. Three children or four. I couldn't decide. Not a white wedding, you wouldn't want it.'

'Then you can wake up,' Lydia said coldly. And it was her turn to go on at Syb. She said she knew what Syb had done. 'Of course you do,' Syb said. 'I know you know.'

When Lydia stared at her, Syb said, 'For heaven's sake, let's leave it at that. Go on from there. I meant well, awful as it sounds. And you are making a mountain out of it—'

'You are saying that because you feel guilty—'

'Guilty of what? Showing a bit of mother

love? I am usually accused of not showing it! When you are an old maid, or whatever they call them today, you will be sorry for this—this play acting,' Syb stormed, and for the moment Lydia understood why Toby shut his eyes to scenes. Syb looked like a fishwife. An attractive fishwife but noisy, nonetheless. 'A molehill, not a mountain. A mere nothing. I sent him across. You got to know him. Now you want to make a farce of it.'

'How would you have felt,' Lydia demanded, 'if someone had been ordered to pretend an interest in you? To see if there was some spark there they could light—'

'I wouldn't have needed it.' There was silence until Syb said, 'Another thing. The woman who spilled the beans meant to make mischief. Don't be soft, Lydia. Don't give her the satisfaction. May I come and stay with you, next week?'

'Of course.'

'We won't talk about it,' Syb said.

When Syb went to stay with Lydia, Ellie asked if she might be excused from making the trip. No one mentioned Vida. 'Of course,' Syb said. 'There is plenty for you to do. Take in as many plays as you want to see. Museums. Galleries.' She gave Ellie twenty pounds ticket money, as she put it.

Syb fitted in well at the house. Will liked her tremendously. She liked Cherry, and now Duke. Everyone loved Lucy. 'It is you,' Syb told Lydia, 'who stick out like a sore thumb.'

'Ma, you said you wouldn't mention it.'

'Marriage? I am not even thinking about it! It is up to you. I've done my bit,' Syb said, virtuously. 'But all you do is mope round the house, go for walks, drive to the beach, drive to the village. You are not even part of the community there. Is there a Gardening Club? Have you joined the W.I.? If there is a Gilbert and Sullivan Society, you have a pretty voice.'

'Ma, for Pete's sake—'

'Well, that is what you will become if you stay here,' Syb warned. 'It's not a bad thing. I am not decrying it. But not for you, I shouldn't have thought.'

'What do you see for me?'

Syb opened her mouth to say, 'Marriage—' and shut it smartly. Lydia laughed. She said, 'Ma, did you want me?' The sad, cold, little sentence dropped between them. Like a stone.

After a while, Syb answered her. 'Yes, I wanted you. Oh, I admit I haven't turned out much of a mother. But when you were born, I was delighted you were a girl. I could see us photographed in the glossies. *Mrs Toby Farmer and Lydia.* Me beautiful and you enchanting. But then, Toby and I separated. Time passed. You grew up—'

'But not enchanting?'

'Well, not like me,' Syb said honestly. 'You and I are so very different. To be honest, love, I don't know you all that well.'

'Ma—'

'What?'

'Don't try it again.'

Syb knew what she meant. She nodded.

'And Ma, don't go off on a different tack. Don't say, one day, "You remember that pleasant Bartlow? I see in *The Times* he has become engaged". Don't do that just to see if I am jealous.'

Syb promised. To change the subject which, she had to admit, made her feel more than a little ashamed, she said, 'Lydia, what's wrong with the uncle? The old man. Ben. I mean, devoted to Vida.

It isn't normal. Not if one knows Vida.'

Lydia, who thought she should not encourage her mother to talk on these lines, changed the subject herself and talked about Connie Coles. Connie had to postpone her visit by a week but she would be here soon. Syb said she was looking forward to seeing Connie again. 'The old-school bit,' Syb said, and laughed.

But next evening Syb met Ben when she was taking a stroll after tea. The setting was romantic. In fact the same pretty road where Lydia and Duke had talked. Ben sat on the stile. He wore a straw boater, white trousers, an open-necked shirt with cravat. When she saw him first Syb thought he looked like something from a Twenties musical, ready to welcome in song and lyric the neatly-tripping heroine as she came swinging a bunch of dog-daisies. A bit old for the juvenile, she amended, as she neared him. The juvenile's still nimble grandfather.

What he said knocked her cold. When they were near enough for her to smile at him and for him to remove the boater, he said, 'You remind me of my mother.'

'Good God,' Syb said, shattered. She recovered herself fairly well and said that surely his mother was dead. Did he think Syb a ghost, then? Or that she looked depressingly aged? If so, she must do something about it.

'The dress,' he said. 'Long and floating. And the parasol. My mother never walked in the sun without a parasol. At home, I mean. In the garden.'

Syb was relieved. She usually dressed for the occasion. It had been a glorious summer day and now, taking a stroll, she wore a long-skirted dress of sweet pea colours and, of course, the parasol. Lydia had thought it a bit much but was too kind to say so.

Ben jumped down from the stile and looked at the dress. 'What material is it?' he asked. He had a rich vein of curiosity. 'Ben can be nosey,' Vida often said. When Syb said, 'Cotton,' he said, quite simply, 'No wonder I didn't know. Housemaids wore cotton in the summer when I was a boy.'

Syb wasn't certain if this reduced her in rank or not. She said, 'Who was your mother?' and when he told her she was impressed. She had heard of his mother. One of the Beauties of her day. Someone had once said of her she had the longest eyelashes in London. The rubbishy knowledge that comes back to one, Syb marvelled. Then wondered if it was rubbishy. To have such eyelashes? There are worse things to be remembered by.

She looked at Ben. His eyelashes were sparse. Took after his father, no doubt.

'Gone for ever,' she heard him say. 'That way of life.'

There were times when Syb thought it a damn good thing it had gone, when her radical mood was uppermost. But there were times when she knew she would have enjoyed it, would have been as selfish as anyone.

'You are a deliciously pretty woman,' he said.

And you are a handsome old cove, she thought. She said, more to be polite than anything, to pass a half hour here in this pleasant spot, 'Do you remember much about the old days?'

Afterwards, when things turned out as they did, she often thought back to this place, this time. When she did, the scene was engraved on her mind like a picture on a calendar, rich in colour, sweetness, and charm.

And a wild leap for Syb out into the future she so much wished for.

Who would have guessed it would turn out like this, a stroll down a country road while waiting for Cherry Matthews to cook a meal?

Eight words. No great sum. They gave her all she wanted, changed her life. And this was the point where she shivered. It always happened. She turned cold and shivered and felt prickles on her arm when she wondered what would have happened if she had stayed in and helped Cherry with the meal, as she had offered. 'You go out,' Cherry had said. 'I'll manage.'

Syb said, 'You must have a fund of stories. You should cash in on them.'

'Write them, you mean? Alec suggested that,' Ben said. And added as testily as he had done to Alec, 'I could never do that. Too much trouble, sitting down scribbling. I don't know how these writer johnnies do it.'

And for a moment Syb asked herself if there was not something about that house that made the two males there so lazy, so lacking in endeavour? Vida was no Circe but the men she looked after couldn't be lazier. A woman, Syb told herself briskly, would have a collection of reminiscences in hardback, long ago, particularly with nostalgia like weeds all over the literary scene.

'Well, don't you give—shall we say, private recitals?' she teased with her charming sun-on-water glittering smile. She knew what the answer would be but she wanted to hear it. 'I mean, surely Vida is interested? Most women would be.'

He said no, Vida didn't want to listen. So Syb said, *'Tell me.'*

She said no more for this was the moment when the idea came to her, so perfect an answer to what she sought, that of course she was suspicious of it, suspicious, now it had happened, at the revelation. She murmured aloud, 'I wonder—' and heard Ben say, 'Now you sound like my mother.'

'I do?'

'Yes. She used to say that. In just that throaty tone "I wonder—" she would say.'

'What did she wonder about?'

'Lovers,' he said simply, and explained. 'Or those who claimed they were in love with her. I was a precocious lad. I should have known nothing. I knew most of what went on. I listened to gossip in the servants' hall and I kept my eyes open.' The best thing about him, she thought, is that he doesn't sound defiant. He is just describing what he was like.

'Go on,' he said.

But then he came to himself. 'I could recognize the overtures,' he said. 'I don't know,' primly since he was, after all, discussing his mother, 'how far it went.'

You old fraud, Syb thought, indulgently. If you don't know, the rest of us do, for there were others who wrote their memoirs and your mother's name has a habit of cropping up, lovely creature that she was.

'But some man would bring her flowers,' Ben said. 'White roses, she loved. And camellias. He would call. In the afternoon. I usually hid behind the potted palms. They were neatly grouped. And he might declare his feelings for her. She would smile. When he had gone, she always did the same thing—'

'Rose and crossed to the mirror and looked at herself and smiled,' Syb said.

'How do you know?'

'It is what I should have done.'

'Yes,' he said. 'It is what she did. And she murmured, "I wonder?" in just that

266

throaty way you did, and she laughed. Then I suppose she went off to dress for the evening. Dinners. Balls. Night after night. During the Season.'

'Talking of dinner,' Syb said, 'will you dine with us tonight? Lydia would be pleased. Mrs Matthews is a splendid cook.'

'Dear lady,' he said, 'it's Tuesday.'

She looked at him.

'I was told not to forget Tuesday,' he explained. 'Vida is cooking a special meal. *Coq-au-vin.*'

Syb just looked at him. He said, after a pause, that of course he could telephone Vida and say he would not be home for dinner. 'Do that,' she said. And gave no indication how the thought delighted her. She waited for him to say he was not dressed for dinner at a friend's house but one thing about Ben, he had believed all his life that people sought his company, not the figure he cut.

While he telephoned Vida, Syb left the door open so that she could hear. Ben explained where he was, that he had been asked to a meal and accepted. Yes, he knew it was Tuesday. Yes, he knew what Vida had promised. But he was sorry. He could not be there. He would be late

267

home, he expected.

He very much enjoyed his meal with Syb and Lydia, Cherry and Duke. The latter left for their own flat. Lydia left. Syb seemed in no hurry to go anywhere. Ben drank Lydia's good brandy and he talked. How he talked. But Syb only encouraged him.

When he did leave, she was too excited to sleep. She went into Lydia's room. Lydia, propped against pillows, was reading.

'You look lonely,' Syb said. Then she went to sit at the dressing-table stool and looked at herself in the mirror. 'I was born out of my time. I am certain of it,' she said. 'What a man. What a catch—'

'Mother—' Lydia sat upright, the book dropped on to the bed beside her. She seldom called Syb mother except in times of stress. 'You don't mean you want *to marry him?*'

'It would spoil it,' Syb said, smiling. 'Lydia, do you find him interesting?'

'He did go on—'

'I have struck gold,' Syb told her. 'Good night, darling. When Connie comes over, may she come straight here?'

'I told you *coq-au-vin,*' Vida said. 'I

go to the trouble of preparing it. Your favourite dish. You go for a stroll and come home at midnight. I didn't know you were going to dine there.'

'I didn't know, myself. I met her in the lane and the next thing I was sitting at her daughter's dinner table.'

'She isn't Morgan le Fay,' Vida raged, beside herself with annoyance.

Sympathetic, though, Ben told himself. Even more sympathetic than my mother appeared to be to those young men.

'She carries me back—' he said aloud.

'What?'

'In time. Do you know, when I first saw her walking towards me in that dress—cotton, she said it was—I thought she was my mother. I told her so.'

'Your mother?' When she rightly grasped this, Vida brayed with laughter. It was some small release. Syb to be taken for Ben's mother. 'What did she say?'

He smiled. He has gone off his head, Vida thought. He looks besotted. Ben said Syb didn't mind. 'Not when she knew who my mother was.'

Vida grew more irritated by the minute. She didn't know what had come over Ben. She could swear he didn't even look the same. He looked as if someone had put a spell on him. Maybe Morgan le Fay, after all. Even his accent seemed different. There was a drawl that wasn't there before. 'Well, be here for dinner tonight,' she ordered. He said he was sorry. He had promised to dine again at the top of the hill. 'This time,' he said, 'I really must change out of flannels and a cravat. I felt a bit of a fool but they were all quite charming. Duke has changed,' he said. 'Not the same feller. Seems a bit fatter, even. Nice little girl, his wife.'

Toby came in. Vida decided to punish Ben. 'I do declare Ben has fallen under Syb's spell,' she said. 'We shall be losing him to that house up there. Well, of course,' Vida said, 'there is more money there for entertaining.'

'Nice woman, Syb,' Toby said, addressing Ben, who nodded.

'Ben told her she reminded him of his mother,' Vida said.

'Now, there was a woman,' Toby told her. 'Where is that portrait Sargent did of her? Sold to America, was it? What a shame. Have a drink.'

Ben did dine at Lydia's that evening

and every evening that week, throwing Vida into a rage of jealousy. She was a possessive woman to whom it was agony to go through something like this. It was impossible for her to share anything or anyone. She even tried tears to keep Ben at home. She said everything except that he could not serve God and Mammon.

A week later, Connie Coles arrived. Syb told her what was in her mind, commanded her to say little at table but to listen hard. Connie said, 'You never give up, do you?'

Lydia, who had been taken into her mother's confidence, also said little. Syb was the feed-man and she had little to do. Once Ben was started, he could go on for hours. And what man would not, facing an audience of three attractive women in the drawing-room after dinner, brandy at his side, cigars for the smoking.

By the Lord Harry, Lydia had to tell herself, I believe Ma is right. I believe she and Connie could pull this off. She has found a treasure trove. Like something hidden away for years in a box in the attic. Ben Bartlow. Vida's poor Ben.

So you may lose Ben as well as Ellie, she mentally addressed Vida. It has been a bad year for you. Your world has cracked right open.

And when Syb and Connie had milked Ben dry, would he go back to Vida? Lydia had come to suspect that Ben Bartlow was a very thick-skinned gentleman indeed. He might try. Would Vida take him back? She didn't know.

When Ben left, Syb said, 'Well, Con, well? What do you think?'

The out-spoken Connie agreed that there was indeed a lot of nostalgia about. 'I'm not surprised, considering the times we live in. I don't go along with it, never having been one for looking back—'

'But if we can make something of it?' Syb said eagerly. 'Oh, not until we've thoroughly explored it and make certain we don't get egg on our faces for trying.'

'You can say that again,' said the professional, grimly.

'But let's try, Con. After all, most women go to the theatre to escape. I don't blame them. They want to look at lovely clothes and hear witty lines. "Was that what it was like?" they ask themselves, and even when they are being sensible and telling themselves it couldn't have been like that for everyone, of course not, they go on to tell themselves that since they are in the theatre, at a matinee, they will enjoy it. And they do. Think, Con, how we shall look. Taffeta, lace, osprey feathers. Roses, camellias, potted palms.' Was she remembering the confessions of a man who had been a precocious small boy, hiding behind the palms? If so, it was only to congratulate him. 'I sat next to a girl at *The Importance of Being Earnest,*' Syb said. 'When Gwendolen entered in Act one, this girl turned to me and said, "I could pinch that hat right off her head and wear it". She looked as if she had never owned a hat in her life. Connie, it will work! A small theatre. A limited season. And I'll back it.'

Still, Connie was not wholly convinced.

Syb soldiered on. 'We'll go to Monte Carlo or Cannes. Take him with us. There should be atmosphere there. Or Baden. Or Marienbad.'

'Cook's Tour for 1906—' Connie said.

'Ben will talk and Ellie will take it all down. Then we can read it. In cold print. Or typescript—'

'It may not stand cold print,' Connie told her.

'Right,' Syb said. 'Right.' She rose to

leave them. 'It was just an idea. But Wilde could come back from the grave and write a play just for you, Connie, and you would hum and ha. Forget it. You can go back tomorrow.'

'You won't get anywhere if you give up so easily,' Connie had the nerve to say. 'Perhaps I haven't lived with it as you have. I can't see it like you can. But I'm willing to be convinced. Let's take the old boy to Cannes. Or Baden. Or wherever. But Syb—'

'What?'

'Why stop with his mother and her pals?'

Syb stared at her.

'Carry it through,' Connie said. 'Start with the Edwardians. Go to the Twenties. Finish with them—us—in old age. We could still be discussing what had happened to those we knew in the dear days of cucumber sandwiches and cedars. Audiences like to follow things through. They are a nosey lot.'

'You are hooked! You have been all the time. You'll go through with it—' Syb flung her arms round Connie and kissed her.

'Perhaps,' Connie said. 'Perhaps. There's a lot to be done.'

'Oh, Con, you know it will be all right. It will be like that sketch in school—'

'If it flops,' Connie said, 'I shall wish you had been expelled that time they threatened it.'

Lydia wished she had a modicum of their enthusiasm for having a go, as Syb would call it. But their enthusiasm was not infectious. She felt very much odd woman out. By the time they did at last go to bed, Syb and Connie had decided upon Monte Carlo.

'Monte Carlo?' Vida screeched. It was the following day and Ben had just told her he would be leaving on a holiday to Monte Carlo. She was baking. She all but raised the rolling pin to hit him. If he had said he was training to be an astronaut she could not have been more astonished. 'You are going to Monte Carlo? Where will you get the money?' She wanted to say it was small enough, the sum he paid to stay here, how was he going to lash out on a trip to the South of France?

'I am being treated,' he said, and explained. This was when her hand tightened on the rolling pin. Ben still had not been let in on the reason why Syb was so anxious for him to go on regaling her with reminiscences. But he didn't say, 'Haven't you had enough?' Not Ben. He was a conceited old man and he was enjoying himself. He had never had such an audience before. He took advantage of it. And now, with her friend Connie, Syb has asked him to go to Monte Carlo. He had accepted instantly. He said he hadn't been there since the Twenties.

'And you recall what it was like?' Syb asked.

'Good lord, yes. As if it were yesterday,' he told her without boasting.

Connie, she thought, we are in!

'They said they would like to take me along,' Ben told Vida. 'Good of them, isn't it?' He added, with awful humorousness, 'You will probably be glad to be rid of me for a bit.'

'For a bit? You will be coming back?' she said.

The sarcasm was lost on Ben. He said of course.

'I never knew you to be sly, before,' Vida accused him. 'Though it isn't your fault. You are just easily led. It's those two up there. Mother and daughter. Tarred with the same brush. They hate me—'

'They never mention you,' he protested.

'They want me to be left here childless, friendless. After all I've done for you,' Vida told him as she would. 'I've taken you in and cared for you. I've let you appear one of the family. Nothing has been too much trouble.' *Coq-au-vin,* she thought. 'All right, go to Monte Carlo. Gamble. Lose your money, the little you have. Come back destitute, like a beggar. And I suppose you will have the nerve to knock at the door and say hallo, Vida.'

He wondered what else one could say. He said he was sorry she was upset. It was just a holiday. He hadn't had a holiday in years. He said Ellie was coming, too.

That did it. Vida started to cry and was still crying when Ben tiptoed from the room. He started packing. He was looking forward to going to Monte Carlo. But he hoped there would be room for him here when he came back.

15

It would not be fair to say that Lydia was depressed when the coterie left for the South of France, and certainly she was not angry as Vida was. She told herself it might be better for her if she could feel something, depression or anger, because then she would have to take a stand and fight against it.

If she felt like anything, she thought it was a cake that had sagged in the centre. There was nothing she wanted to do, nowhere she wanted to go. She tried to rally herself but it was no good. If she could feel something forcefully, she told herself, it might help. She tried to bring to mind the names of the seven Deadly sins, wondering if anything among them sounded worth trying. She never did make a full list but decided that Anger and Gluttony and Avarice did not appeal. Maybe Sloth was what she suffered from?

It was Duke who found her a job.

At dinner, they were discussing, as they

did most days, Syb and her ambitious plan for staging a two-woman show. Syb had written to say things were going well. Connie was cautiously pleased. 'More with the Twenties bit than the Edwardian,' Syb wrote. 'I know why. She was a Twenties figure. Flat-chested with that beaky look they had when they didn't look vacuous. We end in the Forties with the war on. I think it will work,' Syb said. 'What we want is to breathe life into the characters, not a charade. Pray for me.'

Indeed Lydia did. With Syb content, there was less danger of her interfering in Lydia's life.

'I understand Ben is pouring out stories,' Lydia said. 'As fast as Ellie can take them down. I wish there was something I could do.'

'Can you cook?'

'She isn't bad,' Cherry said honestly. Cherry was a superb cook so even this praise was something, and Lydia looked grateful. It came into her mind how few times anyone praised her. And that, she told herself, is because you do nothing for them to praise.

'There's a job going at Will's school,'

Duke said. 'Trendy told me.' The headmaster, Trendham-Smith, had been at Oxford with Duke. 'I met him at the shop today. He looked a bit down and I asked what was wrong. He said the cook has eloped with a Hungarian.'

'Who else?' Lydia said. 'If one elopes, it must be with a Hungarian.'

'Trendy can't get a cook for love nor money. His wife is due to have their third baby, any minute. If you could fill in, Lydia, I am sure that any future family you have, sons I mean, would have free tuition there when they were ready. It wouldn't be your life's work, a cook, but it might fill in the days.'

When Lydia hesitated, 'And don't let your conscience trouble you that you would be taking the bread out of someone's mouth,' Duke said. 'As I said, Trendy has no offers. He is at his wits' end.'

'You've told him about me?' Lydia said, but before Duke could reply there was a telephone call for Lydia from Mr Trendham-Smith himself. He had a charming voice and a persuasive manner so that in no time at all she had promised to help.

'Do you think you should have done

it?' Cherry asked her husband who told her what Lydia needed was a shove in some direction, any direction, rather than mope around the house. 'Maybe,' Duke said, 'Trendy has a brother who will be there on Sports Day. Yes,' he told her before she asked, 'I've put in for a day off. You and I, my love, will stroll on the lawns and beneath immemorial elms, if they have them, with the other parents. We will cheer Will on in the egg-and-spoon but try to persuade him to leave out the sack race since Will would be none too good in harness! I have been approached to play for the fathers' team. Slow bowler.'

'Oh, Duke—' Life had little more it could offer Cherry. Duke in the fathers team, Will in the egg-and-spoon race. But, 'It's a funny old world,' she told herself. 'Me there in my best hat. Lydia sweating it out among the tea urns and the scones, the jam and the cream.'

Interviewed by Trendham-Smith and the pretty young woman he introduced as his missus, Lydia was putty in his experienced hands. She promised to come, next day. There was help in the kitchens in the person of a young girl from the village who, while active, had no wish to take on responsibility. Her cry was, 'I should be no good if anything went wrong.' Nothing did go wrong. After her first day, when she was certain it would be her last, Lydia managed and found she enjoyed it. The missus was delighted and went into hospital and produced her third daughter.

Will didn't know what he thought. He was glad the boys had finished asking personal questions such as, 'Where do you live?' These had been got over early and Will was relieved. He didn't know if he was a snob or not but like most small boys he was a great traditionalist, a stickler for the conventions, and he was glad he didn't have to say he lived with the cook. On the other hand, he might have expected great things from Lydia. School meals remained the same.

'You will be all right for Sports Day? Of course you will,' Trendham-Smith asked Lydia. 'We are thinking of calling the baby Lydia. Did you know? My wife wants you for god-mother.'

Just as well, she thought, he didn't say, 'And you will be here next term, won't you?' She might have nodded. But he had engaged a cook for next term.

Cherry took a hand at cake-making for Sports Day. Scones, sponges, jam tarts. Sandwiches were piled high. It was a scorching day. Iced tea. Lemonade. Ice cream. The older boys carried it out and it seemed to the provider, there in the kitchen, that ravenous hordes must be waiting, outside the back door, for no sooner were the boys out than they were in again, beaming, holding empty trays.

But at last tea was over and Lydia found time to drink a cup herself, to share with Myra, the village maiden, the plate of cakes they had cunningly hidden, put on lipstick, smooth down her hair, shed her white overall, and say, 'I'm going to see what's going on. You coming?'

'Not me. I'll stay here, put my feet up. But you go. You ought to be out there, anyway.'

'Why?'

'Well, you belong, don't you?' Inevitably, Myra turned everything she said into a question. 'Makes more sense, don't it? You out there, not in the kitchen. You should be shouting for your own kid or looking at his pipe-rack.'

Shouldn't I? Perhaps so, Lydia agreed. She liked the school, she had enjoyed

284

helping out. She liked the staff and she adored the small boys. As she searched in the woodwork room for Will's pipe-rack she did wish she had someone like Will belonging to her. She wasn't doing much about it, she thought.

Here was the pipe-rack. The work of *William Matthews*.

Duke had said pridefully that Will would be the first Prime Minister to have made his own pipe-rack. She hoped Cherry was enjoying herself. Cherry had made herself a new dress for the occasion. Blue cotton with a huge straw hat trimmed with cornflowers. Lucy, who was here too, was dressed in a pint-size replica.

I want a daughter too. Like Lucy.

She left the school rooms and went outside. The first person she saw was Alec Bartlow.

He was walking away from her. She stayed where she was and watched him. He was escorting a very pretty young woman dressed in a long black and white striped silk skirt, a white blouse and a straw boater of the shape Ben affected, only it had black ribbons at the back. Oh, very smart, Lydia told herself. Chic, no less. A bit much for a school Sports Day? No need to carp, she ordered. With that fair hair and that lovely face she could get away with anything. For the girl had paused for a moment and turned back to look behind her. And in that moment Lydia learned her face by heart. Then she turned, put her arm through Alec's, and they went on together.

Matey, it looked.

Lydia found herself thinking that old, well-worn thought. It hadn't taken him long to find someone else.

Strange, she thought, I don't normally use such phrases, a bit common, certainly pedestrian, but when certain things happen to you, you don't stop to think how the words sound. You just have to get them out. To ease what is festering and boiling within you. *Jealousy.*

The good old green-eyed monster. Alec and the pretty girl disappeared in the direction of the cricket field. Lydia had meant to watch the match. She couldn't, now.

What an escape, she breathed. If I had come out a few seconds earlier we should have come face to face. She thanked the Lord in His wisdom while beseeching Him that the pretty woman was a not a widow or divorced with a son at the school. Alec is quite likely to marry her. A ready-made family. Like Duke.

I bet she wouldn't refuse him if he proposed by the elephant house at the Zoo, or anywhere. Please, her prayer went on, don't let him propose, if he will propose to her, at the Zoo.

She returned to the kitchen. Myra was asleep. Lydia crept away and went home. At least, she kept telling herself, I have found out that I am human. I can give a date and the hour when I found out that cold fish, Lydia Farmer, was human.

Jealousy ate into her and made her miserable, made her wish she could have back that afternoon at the Zoo when, she realized now, she had refused a man she should have said yes to. She loved the man. She must love him, after all, to feel as she did. Oh, she knew she loved him. Then why had she acted as she did? Because she was stupid. Syb had been right. And, as Syb had said, when she was an old maid she would regret what she had done. She regretted it now. No need to wait until she was an old maid.

She asked Cherry, later, if Cherry had seen Alec at the school. She hoped her voice held just the right tone of light interest.

'Duke met him.' The kind Cherry didn't say any more because Duke had told her Alec was with a corker of a girl, a smasher.

'He was escorting a very attractive girl,' Lydia said. She described to a detail the black and white outfit. Oh, my poor love, Cherry thought.

Duke, when he returned, was able to give them details. Her name was Mrs Darcy. She was a widow. She had a small boy at the school. Her husband had been killed some years ago in an aircrash.

It was to Lydia's credit that she did not look ceilingwards and accuse God of letting her down. Duke went on to say Mrs Darcy lived in Paris with her mother.

'And where does Alec come in?' Cherry asked.

Duke didn't know. Alec had introduced him to the lovely Mrs Darcy but that was all. Neither Cherry nor Duke looked at Lydia.

'Mrs Darcy might, she just might, be Alec's cousin,' Cherry advanced.

'Pigs,' Lydia said, 'might fly.'

Two days later it was the end of

term. She said goodbye to the school. Trendham-Smith and his missus gave her a nineteenth-century print of the school when it had been the local manor house. 'Don't forget us,' he said, but whether he was touting for custom in case she found herself the mother of boys, Lydia didn't know.

I shall go to London, Lydia thought. From there I may leave for Ceylon. Or Burma. Anywhere where there are elephants.

But before she could take this step Toby had a request to make.

She was alone in the house. Duke and Cherry and the children had left for a holiday in Wales. They had asked Lydia to go with them but she had only shaken her head. If she went, she would be like a maiden aunt, she would be playing gooseberry. Without her, Duke and Cherry and the children would be a family. With her, they would feel they had to include her in everything. 'I know what you are thinking and it is a nonsense,' Cherry had said. 'But if you have made up your mind, I know nothing will change it. Lydia, do you wish you had never come here? To Wadden.' To the house below, she meant.

'No. At least I stirred things up a bit.' For you, she thought, and for Duke. For Ellie. Even for Ben.

And made a right mess of my own life. As I have said, the sum total of what I have learned is that I am human. It took me twenty-five years, a good education and much travelling as well as returning to base to learn this!

On this hot summer day, it surprised her to open the door and find Toby there. He came in, welcomed the coolness of her sitting-room, refused to sit on the verandah, accepted a drink. He might have commented on the way she had arranged the room, since he had never seen it before, but not Toby. He stretched in her most comfortable chair and thanked her when she brought the drink. When he felt he was able to start a discussion without unduly wearing himself out, he said, 'I am sick and tired of that place below.'

'But you don't want to move here, surely?' she said, surprised. If he did, Vida would be after her, Lydia, with a broomstick. To take Ellie away was bad enough. And Ben. But Toby. Vida would never let Toby leave.

She was relieved to see him shake his head. She thought she heard him say he wanted to go on safari but decided she couldn't have. But then he said, 'Kenya—' so she supposed she had been right. She felt she should tell him, straightaway, that going on safari, romantic as it sounded, did involve personal physical exercise. You might hire your white hunter, hire guides and transport, and the rest, but you yourself must needs join in or the whole thing wasn't worth it. You could not, as it were, go on safari by proxy. And the days of being carried on a litter through African terrain were over. A pity. Toby would have enjoyed it.

'I've always wanted to go to Kenya,' he said. 'No shooting, mind. Not ever. Not anywhere. I couldn't live with those sad-eyed, reproachful-looking stuffed heads above me on the wall, telling me that if it wasn't for my sort they might still be nipping over the bush or the plains. We've got a nerve,' Toby said, 'to shoot animals, do our damnedest to exterminate them, when we make such a mess of our own world.'

There were times, she thought, when she loved Toby.

He invited her to go with him to Kenya. She equated this, probably truthfully, with asking her to pay for it.

When she shook her head, he did look momentarily put out. 'Why not? Nothing to keep you here.'

'Maybe I don't fancy myself in khaki drill and a pitch helmet.'

'You would look good in it.'

She might go to look at elephants at close quarters. But now she didn't think so. She could always see her favourites at the Zoo.

She wondered where Alec was at the moment. And thinking of him made her think of Mrs Darcy so that resolutely she listened harder to what her father had to say. But he only said, 'Oh, come on.'

'I'll pay for you to go. You and Vida,' she said.

There was silence. Toby shut his eyes, his old trick. Did he hope that if he kept them shut, she would say, 'Oh, all right, not Vida.'

He said at last, 'I don't know what has got in to Vida, these days. Nag, nag. She is a pain. She used to be a bright little thing. Bouncy. That was part of her charm. But now—'

'Yes?'

'She just wants to put the clock back,' he said.

'To before I came?'

He looked at her and grinned. 'Maybe. She keeps saying things have changed since you came to stay.'

'Ellie would have gone, anyway.'

'Ellie. Bartlow,' Toby agreed. 'Vida hates change. She does her nut about moving a piece of furniture. Pushing it here and back again. Drives you frantic. So I want to get out for a bit.'

To let her push furniture around in an empty house? He really is one of the most selfish men. A minute ago I warmed towards him. Now I think him hateful. And yet I can't say, 'Poor Vida.' She never could be sorry for Vida. But a glimpse of what life was like with Toby was enough to make you wonder how Vida endured him. She really must love him.

She poured him another drink. It would be bad taste to say, 'Dad, what would you have done if you had to earn a living?' but she was tempted.

But she did say, 'Dad, did you enjoy the war? Some people use the word.'

'Not enjoy it,' he said. 'Don't they say

war is three-quarters boredom and the rest action?'

Maybe that one quarter exhausted you for the rest of your life, she thought. But she also knew that Toby's war had not been inactive. His M.C. wasn't won for finding some ways of escaping boredom.

'I'm lucky,' she heard him say. 'I never had many problems. Syb might have become a problem but she left.'

And I might have proved one but I was never there.

'Syb was generous,' Toby said. 'And Vida is a good housekeeper.'

'Dad, don't you have any feelings?'

He looked at her and laughed. 'When I saw what having feelings did for Syb, I reckoned I couldn't afford them. Not both of us. Do you have feelings?'

'I'm human.' Though it isn't all that long since I found this out.

She said, 'Take Vida with you and I'll give you the money for the trip. It would break her heart to be left behind.' Vida will hate Africa, every minute of it. But she will hate more being without Toby. (She will never believe that I laid down this condition).

'Ellie is in Monte Carlo with Syb,' Toby

said. 'And Bartlow is with them. What are they up to?'

Lydia told him.

'Syb has wanted something like that, all her life,' Syb's ex-husband said. 'An outlet for her historic leanings. I'll go up for the First Night.' Then he sighed. 'I'll ask Vida, then. But the plan was to get away from Vida for a bit.'

'Africa?' Vida repeated. 'Safari? Wild animals? There are safari parks in this country if you want to see wild animals. Or the Zoo where they are safe behind bars. I am not going to Africa. It's Lydia. She has put you up to this.'

'Lydia knew nothing about it until I went to her and told her I would like to go. She'll stake me. Well, not stake,' Toby admitted. 'She'll give me the trip as a present. Good girl, Lydia. Generous. I'm asking you to come,' he told Vida. 'And I don't intend to ask you twice. Say yes or no. But don't make a scene. There has been no peace in this house, this year.'

'Of course not. Not since Lydia came. She has broken up the pattern. The pattern of a happy home. Ellie has gone. Ben has gone.'

'Don't you like Lydia?' Toby asked. To say the least, it sounded naïve. But then, Toby was not all that observant. But his words gave Vida a chance to draw breath, as it were, and speak more reasonably, something she always found hard when Lydia's name was mentioned. 'She is a force for change, that girl, for all she looks as if butter wouldn't melt in her mouth!'

'I wish you wouldn't say these things.'

'Why not? Everyone says them. It's a well-known phrase—'

Toby groaned and kept his eyes shut.

Vida continued. 'Not everyone likes change. I don't. I'm conservative-minded. I like things to develop in their own time. I could see Ellie happily married to some nice local boy, living not far away. I could have my share of the grand-children, then. I didn't think Ben would end up in Monte Carlo. Sometimes he would talk about it but I used to stop him. I didn't think it was good for him.'

'Not good for him?' He opened his eyes now, and stared at her.

'Thinking of what had happened when he was young and had some money. When he compared that with what he is today.'

Merciful heavens, he thought, you see

what you want to see. And what you want to see are battery hens. Vida, he thought, Lydia is right but not for the reason she gave. You need Africa. The size may do something for you and to you.

'Well?' he said. She knew what he meant. Tears dropped on to her sewing. But at last she said, for she could not endure the thought of three months here on her own without Toby, 'I'll come.'

'Not on sufferance, mind. Try to enjoy it.'

'Where will I get the right clothes?'

'Ask Lydia.'

She would die first. I'll ask Amalie. Thinking of Amalie being told that Vida was going out to Kenya for three months' safari did bestow a weak ray of sunshine. Amalie would be jealous. Amalie didn't come here much now, now that Duke was gone. That's another thing, Vida thought, rage suddenly sprouting again, gushing through her. If Lydia hadn't helped him deceive my sister, she would still be with Duke. She forgot, for the moment, the times she had wished Amalie herself would get rid of Duke.

'Toby?'

'Yes?'

'What about the house?'

'What about it?'

'Who will look after it?'

'Lydia, if you ask her.'

'Sometimes,' Vida said with a sudden dignity, 'sometimes, I think you say things just to annoy me.'

She would not ask Lydia to look after the house. When we come back, heaven knows how it will look.

Oh, there were problems. 'Toby, what about Ben?'

'Nothing wrong with Ben.'

'He may want to come back and we shan't be here.'

'Then he can make a willow cabin at your gate,' Toby said, half remembering something he had once learned. But he said, 'Ben may not come back, he may not want to. Ben is on to a good thing.'

'What do you mean?'

'Didn't he tell you?'

'You mean that nonsense about what his mother did, that sort of thing? Syb being interested. Does that make him a male Scheherazade?' Vida demanded. 'Syb won't listen to that sort of thing for a thousand and one nights or however long it is! Sometimes,' she said crossly, 'I don't know what you are talking about.'

So he told her. He told her Syb hoped there was material in what Ben remembered to fill a script for a show she and Connie Coles planned to put on.

'An amateur show?'

'Professional.'

'Syb—an actress? She has had no training.'

'Well, I don't think she will fall flat on her face,' Toby said. 'She'll give it all she's got. And she is a beautiful woman. She will look delicious. I think they will be successful. The Edwardians. It's a period most people like. Women, anyway. It must be the hats.'

'I don't hanker after it. It think it absurd to hanker after something that will never come again. Besides,' Vida said, 'it wasn't so good for domestics.'

Oh, spare a thought for domestics, Toby agreed silently. Take the opposite view to Syb. Because if you had lived then you would have taken your whack out of the domestics, by God you would.

But Vida was smouldering because she thought Ben had let her down. If he were here she could have made his presence an excuse for staying at home to look after him. They had all let her down, she thought. Which was what happened to people who gave every moment of their time to others, not counting the cost. Perhaps, though, Ben would be back before they left. You could not arrange a trip to Africa as you would to Southend. Surely Ben would get tired of Syb and her friend, or they of him, more likely. 'When do we leave?' she enquired, and was heartbroken to hear Toby say, 'Next week.'

He went on, 'I made the arrangements before I went to see Lydia. I booked for two because I thought she might come with me. She wouldn't. She insisted I take you.' He said, 'Now, be quiet, Vida.'

But before they left for Africa, Toby found the energy to climb the hill a second time, to thank Lydia, he said, in case he had not seemed sufficiently grateful, last time. She was touched. She said, 'Dad, I am going to make arrangements to give the house to you.' When she said it, she looked at him and she wouldn't have sworn he wasn't thinking, 'Must you? A house is a responsibility. Things work out all right as they are.'

But Lydia meant what she said. She had

been thinking about it for some time. If anything happened to Toby, she did not want Vida to have nowhere to live or Vida smarting under the assumption she was only living in her beloved house by courtesy of Lydia. 'I don't want to live there,' she said aloud.

And Toby said, 'It didn't work out the way you thought it would, did it? No bosom of the family, that sort of thing?'

'No.'

'You romantics,' he scoffed but kindly. 'The rest of us don't make it easy for you. You're a nice daughter to have, though. Syb did a good job on you.'

'She doesn't think so. She thinks I should marry.'

'And she is right. You aren't a career woman. Are you,' he said, 'one skin short?'

As might be expected, she looked her surprise. Toby explained. 'Nothing worse in a woman than being one skin short. Makes her a damn' bore. Always weeping, finding slights where none were intended. You aren't, are you, Lydia?'

'I hope not.' But as she said it she wondered if Alec did not find her a one-skin short woman? For the moment she felt terrible in case he did. And surprised at Toby's acumen. She said so. 'I didn't know you were so perceptive.'

'If I sit with my eyes shut, I am not always asleep. I may not appear to face up to things but I usually know what is going on and why. You are not a facer-upper, either. Or you wouldn't have stayed with Vida longer than a week.'

16

Amalie, when asked by Vida if she would go up occasionally to keep an eye on the house, said no, she would not go within a hundred miles of it. This annoyed Vida. 'You were glad enough to come, once.' She said cruelly, 'You won't see anything of that man, if that is what is worrying you. He has a job in Wadden. I never see him. I don't go into the bookshop much,' Vida said truthfully. 'I hear,' she said, 'they are very happy.' She had not heard it but was intent on annoying Amalie. 'I expect she will start a family soon.' Amalie rang off.

So Vida made arrangements with her daily woman to see to things. 'Africa?' her woman said. 'I've been there. Tangiers. We went last year. That's Africa, isn't it?'

Vida nodded, not bothering to say it wasn't all that near where she was going. Vida couldn't bear the thought of going to Kenya. Each day away from home would be purgatory. It didn't help when the Daily said it was a long way to go just to see lions. There were lions at Longleat. Vida would have preferred Longleat.

Perhaps it was as well she did not know that Toby gave Lydia a key to the house, telling her he would be happier to know that she could keep an eye on things. 'I didn't know you cared,' she teased. He didn't say he did or he didn't. When he told the Daily, commanding her at the same time not to tell Vida, she said, 'Don't get on, do they? You can see it in her face—Mrs Farmer's. Right, I'm glad she's got a key. I may not always be able to come so I'll telephone your daughter and she can see to things.'

Toby should have warmed to her. Like him, she did not believe in wearing herself out for others.

So they left, Toby and Vida. Vida, petty to the last, made certain she did not say goodbye to Lydia.

I have the stage to myself, Lydia thought. Ellie gone, Toby and Vida temporarily absent, Ben still with Syb and Connie.

And what part do I play now? The visitor who came, dallied awhile, then left almost without trace? Vida wouldn't agree with the last bit. She thinks me a tornado.

I am as lonely as before I came.

For heaven's sake, she raged at herself, *shut up*. Stop feeling sorry for yourself. In Cape Town you told yourself things would be better here. Unless you change, nothing will change. It isn't the background. It's you. You weren't even certain, now the play is over, what part you played. Toby's daughter? He didn't want you. Vida's stepdaughter? The same applies, only more so. Ellie? You helped a bit but not as much as Syb was able to do. You are too inclined to wait in the wings, my girl.

Where Syb and Ellie and the rest are prepared to work like beavers for what they want, you wait for life to hand it to you on a plate.

Life did hand it to you. Alec Bartlow asked you to marry him but because of your thin skin (one skin short?) you said no. Oh, Syb did what she did for the best. You say you love her but I am not one hundred per cent certain you have forgiven her. And Alec? He, poor devil, was innocent enough. He did what the charming Mrs Farmer suggested. A lot of men wouldn't have bothered.

But at last she ceased castigating herself for what she had done and not done. There was no future in going on at herself. She didn't think she would wear a hair shirt. If it was foolish pride that had brought her where she was, then she acknowledged it, and that was that. Time now to pick up the pieces.

She rose and looked at her face in the mirror. Nothing there in that cool look to give away the battle that had raged in her mind. Well, good for you, sly puss, she told herself, but Alec Bartlow was in attendance upon a flower of a girl, an enchanting piece, chic, pretty, laughing. And blonde. Perhaps he preferred blondes. Lydia had never asked.

So many things I didn't find out about him.

I could never go to a school sports day wearing a black and white skirt which brushed the grass at my feet, a blouse and a boater. No, she thought, self-pity suddenly welling within her like indigestion. *I* was Cinders in the kitchen. When you saw them together, you should have run after them, shouting, 'Hi, wait a minute. Alec. It's me—'

That's likely, she thought morosely. I'm not that sort of girl. I'm the prim sort.

Prim and jealous of blondes, miserable

and longing for him. If he asked her a third time to marry him, she would say, 'Yes, please. How soon?'

Well, do something about it. Run after him, if that is the only way to get him, but perhaps more subtly than shouting, 'Hi—' Telephone him at the office, tell him you saw him on sports day. Tell him where you were on sports day. Make it into a gay little tale. Then cunningly ask him if he is coming here soon again.

She forced herself to telephone, all ready to chatter lightly and gaily and with intent to find out his plans.

Mr Bartlow was in Paris.

Back down the board, you, she told herself. Down a snake to where you started.

Paris. Mrs Darcy lived in Paris.

Paris is a big city. They need not be together. Paris is a romantic city. If I know Bartlow, he won't waste such a background.

So her thoughts went. It was a wonder she recognized herself.

Duke and Cherry were home now and that night there was a celebration dinner when Duke produced champagne. 'He has had a stroke of luck,' Cherry said. 'An aunt has died and left him some money.'

Lydia did indeed congratulate him. Cherry said there was more to come. This morning, Duke had sold a story.

'You are going it,' Lydia said, delighted for him. He rose, came round the table to where she sat, kissed her. He kissed Cherry on the way back.

Lydia said suddenly, 'Buy this house, why don't you? You like it here. I don't think I shall stay. Tomorrow we can go into the business side of it.' She sounded so offhand, Cherry was alarmed.

'You can't get rid of houses at this rate! You have just given one to your father.'

'I've just said I shan't need a house.'

'Of course you will need a house,' Cherry said. 'Where will you live when you are married?'

'I don't have to carry on Syb's tradition of providing my spouse with a roof,' Lydia said. There was silence. She thought both of them must be wondering about the spouse. So she said brightly, 'I think I shall go on my travels again.'

'I wish you wouldn't say that,' Cherry told her. 'When you say it, it is the saddest thing?'

'Where will you go?' Duke asked.

'Perhaps to see the elephants.' Then Lydia excused herself and left them together. They looked at one another. For each, Lydia's miserable state, for however much she tried to hide it, was just that, was the one cloud on their horizon. They didn't mind the cloud being there as long as they could help shift it. But to help they must understand, and what was this about elephants? This was a new departure.

'Her head may be turned,' Cherry said softly. 'A lot has happened to her lately. Where do they have elephants?'

'Africa.'

'She won't go to Africa. Africa has Vida in it.'

'India, Burma, Ceylon.'

Cherry burst into tears. She said she really could not bear seeing Lydia prepare for yet another Odyssey. 'She came here with such hopes. She has been so good to us, made it easy for us. It should be easy for her.'

'What should?'

'Grabbing Alec Bartlow.'

He said dubiously he didn't see Lydia grabbing anyone. She wasn't the sort.

'Am I the sort? She told me to grab you.'

'So she did.' He kissed her again.

It was all very pleasant but Cherry thought it didn't settle much for Lydia.

Next day, when Lydia said she was going up to London where she might make arrangements to go to Ceylon for a holiday, she had never been there, Cherry said, almost diffidently, that there were elephants, surely, at the London Zoo.

Lydia said she had seen those elephants.

'You must see them in the wild, so to speak?' Cherry ventured. She was out of her depth, she knew she was.

'Not really. It's the Zoo.'

'You don't care for it?'

'I've been there.'

'Oh, Lydia,' Cherry said, 'the grass isn't greener, you know that. Nor the elephants more gorgeous in Ceylon. Don't go. Pay another visit to the Zoo.'

'No.'

'Lydia, Ceylon is too far away.' Too far from him, her tone implied. I don't say he will forget you but he may not chase you to Ceylon.

'He asked me to marry him,' Lydia said. 'At the Zoo,' She paused and said, 'I refused.'

Well, don't blame the Zoo, Cherry

thought. What she said was, 'Don't give up. Keep on trying.'

'I am not a girl who pursues men.'

'Not men. One particular man.'

'I can't get him out of my mind,' Lydia admitted.

'You won't in Ceylon.'

But Lydia went to London though when she got there she did not immediately book to fly to Ceylon.

Something seemed to hold her back from making the trip to the travel agent.

On her second afternoon in London she bought the ark. It was in the children's department of a store. It wasn't bright or new or shiny. It was what might be described as second-hand though Lord knows many loving busy hands had played with it! It was large and well made. It looked as if it really could sail with its precious cargo and bring them safe out of danger. Lydia picked up the hinged half of the roof. Inside it was packed with wooden animals, each well carved, sturdy as the ark itself. Of course she found the elephants almost at once.

The ark was delivered to her at her hotel. She knew she would never part with it. She could imagine children who had played with it, and she could imagine her own children playing with it. Some girls, she thought, still collect sheets and towels, tablecloths, in what is known as a bottom drawer. When they ask me, thirty years on, the first thing I collected for my future home, 'An ark,' I shall say. 'The first time I saw it I knew it was for me and mine.'

Next morning, when she judged Alec Bartlow might be in the office, she telephoned. He was still in Paris.

Later in the day she caught a plane for Paris. She had been given the address where he was staying. And Lydia was winging to Paradise. For in the newspaper she had brought in London there was a picture of the enchanting Mrs Darcy, smiling and holding on to the arm of a beaming, handsome, man who had rescued one Lydia Farmer from despair. They had been married that day, it said, at a registry office in London.

When she arrived at Alec's hotel, she was told he had returned to England that morning. She spent a night in Paris, then left for home herself.

You are chasing him.

By gum.

Then, back in London, the old Lydia took over from the new one, the one who chased Alec. She became, if not apprehensive, diffident. How would it sound if she told him the truth, that she had flown over to Paris to ask him, face to face, if he was going to marry Mrs Darcy. Of course, he would have to tell her not Mrs Darcy now, but there might be a second favourite, a red-head, this time.

So the barriers, the doubts, piled up again. Why can't you be like you were yesterday, she wailed to herself. But that was yesterday, and Paris, and Paris has an effect, makes people act differently. If you are romantic, Paris makes you doubly so. If you are diffident, it gives you courage. All for the sake of love.

But now she was back in London. Prosaic, practical-looking, grey and solid. There was drizzle falling. Not easy here to find oneself airborne, so to speak. One's feet were too firmly fixed to the hard pavement.

So what did one do, she asked herself, and looked at the ark as she asked.

An hour later she went round in person to his office. She did not ask to see him but gave the receptionist a small parcel for him. Then she left. Nothing to betray that she was trembling. But she thought that Syb might be proud of her, if Syb knew. Then she went back to the country.

She had the house to herself. The family were out for the day. She made herself a meal, then in the dusk walked down to the house at the bottom of the hill. She let herself in and did a tour, making certain everything was all right. She could not but wonder what Toby and Vida were doing, at this moment, and how Vida was standing up to Africa.

The place had a ghostly look. Vida had covered the furniture with dust sheets, taken down and stacked pictures and mirrors. So it had the air of a house awaiting Sherman's army.

She sat at the piano and played some tunes. 'Sarie Marais.' 'Cherry Ripe'. The first for the place she had started from. The second, of course, for Cherry.

'Home, Sweet Home.' She grimaced on this one. Well, maybe she hadn't found it yet but it must be around somewhere. This time last year, Cherry and Duke had not met. Look at them now.

Neither had you met Alec. (And look at me now).

She played on. She was enjoying herself.

'One More River'. Thinking of her elephant, the wooden elephant from the ark. 'The animals went in one by one'.

She played 'Rule, Britannia'. and 'The Wedding March'.

'I was hoping for that,' Alec said from the doorway. 'It makes it easier for what I have to say.'

'Like a film,' she said. 'The audience would know you were there. I wouldn't. I go on playing, then you speak and I turn—'

'What do you say?' When she said nothing, he said, 'Don't you go coy on me, again. Lucy has better manners. If Lucy were here and I came in unexpectedly, she would say hallo. At least. She might put her arms round my neck and kiss me. But that's Lucy. Unique.'

Lydia longed to put her arms round his neck, and kiss him. To prove that Lucy was not unique. But she did neither. And she found she could not play another note. Her musical journey was over.

'"Sarie Marais" to "Rule Britannia",' he said 'And a lot in between.'

'Not much. Not much happens to me,'

'You are either too modest or ungrateful.

You had a declaration of marriage,' he said. 'Is that what they call it?'

'A proposal.'

'If you like. I prefer to think I declared myself. And talking of that,' he said, 'I received a declaration, too, this morning. Or a proposal, if you prefer.'

He watched with the greatest of pleasure the red sweep into her face.

He took from his pocket what she had sent him. He had taken it out of the box but it was still wrapped in the paper she had put round it. Carefully he took this off and held in his hand a wooden elephant, a scrap of veiling and orange blossom round its head. A bow round its trunk.

'Where is its mate?'

'At home,' she said. And she told him about the ark she had bought.

'I am right,' Alec said, 'in construing what it means? You have changed your mind?'

She nodded.

'Why?'

'I found out I was human.' She said it honestly and his heart warmed towards her. 'I found it out when I saw you with someone else.'

'Why?'

'Because I thought you were mine! I could, to use a word I haven't used since my childhood and not much then, have scrammed her eyes out. I could have ripped her smart outfit off her back and jumped three times on her hat.'

'Where was this?'

When she told him, he said, 'Duke didn't say you were there. I wish I had known. Fifi and I would have joined you in the kitchen and done our whack buttering the scones.'

'Her name is not—?'

'Fifi? Yes, it is, and it suits her,' he said severely.

'Yes, it suits her. She has a French look.'

'She is as English as fish and chips. I was a friend of her husband's.'

'I thought you were in love with her.'

'I am. Everyone loves Fifi.'

But she wasn't jealous now. Of course everyone loved Fifi. I shall love her myself when I get to know her. I think I should send her a wedding present.

'I went to Paris,' she confessed.

'What for?'

'You want it spelled out?'

'I am a man. I thrive on it.'

'To find you. For I found I simply could not live another day without seeing you and asking you—'

'Yes?'

'If you meant to marry someone else. But I read about Fifi's marriage in the plane on the way over. I was walking on air when I went to your hotel. But you had gone. When we marry,' she said, 'it will be like marrying a courier.'

'I am leaving the firm.'

'Oh no.' Her dismay was obvious. 'You are doing so well there—'

'How do you know that?'

'I should know if you were not. And you give the impression of being happy there without being chased mad by the wild dogs of ambition.'

'I like that,' he said. 'I shall use it myself, if you don't mind. The wild dogs of ambition. Oh, I like to give an honest day's work. I hate short-changing. I enjoyed extending myself if that is the word. But then I couldn't see myself around, any more. In London. When that happens, and it can, one wants to look for a place where one shows up not only to the best advantage to others but satisfactorily to oneself. I am going into partnership with

318

my uncle. An old-fashioned firm in an old-fashioned town. You will like it. I was coming back to ask you to marry me when it was all settled.'

'But I jumped the gun.'

'I shall remember that,' he said happily. 'I think it makes a good foundation for the future.' He said, 'It's time the cookie crumbled your way, love.'

'Pinch me,' she heard herself say. 'I can't really believe it,'

'I'll do better. I'll kiss you.' He did. 'And ask you formally. I know what a girl you are to cross your ts and dot your is—'

'Oh, no. It sounds awful.'

'Lots of habits we grow out of,' he said. 'With six kids to look after. Lydia Farmer, will you marry me and come to live with me and let us put our roots down in that country town I mentioned?' He added gently, 'Come home, Lydia.'

This Large Print Book for the Partially sighted, who cannot read normal print, is published under the auspices of

THE ULVERSCROFT FOUNDATION

THE ULVERSCROFT FOUNDATION

. . . e hope that you have enjoyed this Large Print Book. Please think for a moment about those people who have worse eyesight problems than you . . . and are unable to even read or enjoy Large Print, without great difficulty.

You can help them by sending a donation, large or small to:

**The Ulverscroft Foundation,
1, The Green, Bradgate Road,
Anstey, Leicestershire, LE7 7FU,
England.**

or request a copy of our brochure for more details.

The Foundation will use all your help to assist those people who are handicapped by various sight problems and need special attention.

Thank you very much for your help.